ROUGH COUNTRY. ROUGH JOB.

Quincy came to the mountain country know-ing he could rely only on himself. He knew that putting through a railroad where every man carried a gun to stop him was next to impossible—but if he could only get to Devil's Canyon and hold it, there still was a chance.

DEVIL'S CANYON

E. E. Halleran

BALLANTINE BOOKS • NEW YORK

Library of Congress Catalog Card Number: 56-9289

ISBN 0-345-29433-5

Manufactured in the United States of America

First Edition: April 1956
Fourth Printing: May 1981

Chapter 1

WHEN QUINCY arrived at the Pike Junction depot he was as nearly perfect a dude as he could make himself. The fine gray top hat was brushed until it shone, the linen was snowy-white, the well-tailored trousers were freshly pressed and the handsome frock coat would have been noteworthy on the avenues of New York or Boston. Quincy was practically beautiful—and hated every minute of it.

He timed his long strides so as to arrive at the depot just as the Machete local backed in, hoping that the normal activities of train time would divert attention from him. This ought to be the last day of his masquerade and he didn't want to strain his temper any more than necessary. After a full week of ignoring the ribald comments of fellow passengers, his self-control was wearing pretty thin.

The train caught his attention quickly—a locomotive, a day coach, a baggage car, and eight freight cars of various types, all of them bearing the gilded or painted letters of Rocky Mountain Pacific Railroad. That seemed a bit peculiar. The Machete branch was under lease to R.M.P. from Colorado Midland. Why wasn't R.M.P. using any Midland rolling stock?

He let his glance wander toward the crowded rail yards west of the depot and the question repeated itself. Strings of freight cars were everywhere, most of them loaded with rails, ties or other construction materials. So far as Quincy could see every car belonged to Rocky Mountain Pacific or some foreign road. It didn't add up. Pacific ought to be getting as much use as possible out of Midland equipment.

The local's baggage car had stopped directly in front of him so he moved directly to its open door, swinging his over-sized valise into the car. "Machete," he said. "Here's my ticket."

The baggage man nodded and started to lift the heavy bag. An expression of surprise crossed his features and he contented himself with shoving the valise farther back into the car. "Yes, sir," he said, a measure of respect in the words.

Quincy turned away in a hurry, aware that he had made a mistake. In his dude role he wasn't supposed to be showing off muscles. It was hard enough to make his big rawboned frame look properly foppish without spoiling the effect with any weight-lifting acts. He even tried to slump a little as he walked back toward the day coach, hoping that people would look at his fine clothing and not at the big shoulders that filled out the coat.

By the time he reached the car steps he knew that something had gone wrong with the act. Men were watching him, as usual, but they were not snickering as other men had done all the way from St. Louis. After a week of the masquerade he had learned to recognize the somewhat cautious amusement which his appearance caused. This morning the reaction was different. Maybe the performance with the valise had made them notice his size rather than his garb.

He was still puzzled about it when he took his seat in the grimy old day coach. The half-dozen passengers—construction workers or hardrock miners, he judged—were men who would have not hesitated to rawhide a foppish greenhorn. Now they were keeping pretty quiet, watching him, but without comment. They were hostile rather than scornful and he couldn't quite figure out why.

Then the locomotive tooted a couple of blasts and the train clanked into motion, giving Quincy something else to puzzle over. On the river side of the track were more sidings filled with Colorado Midland rolling stock. In two minutes he counted five locomotives and thirty-odd cars, all of them rusting and in obvious need of repair.

The new question took his mind from the more personal one. He knew that Colorado Midland was suing in the state courts to have the Pacific lease revoked, charging that Pacific had violated the agreement by permitting Midland equipment to deteriorate. Pacific was fighting the suit—yet here they were practically flaunting the evidence that would defeat them. Quincy wanted to know why.

Five minutes later he added another question to his list. As the train dragged westward up the bank of Boulder River he noticed a repair crew working on the track. Hurrying to the rear of the car he spent several minutes in a close scrutiny of the roadbed. It was good trackage all along the line and in two places he saw other crews at work, one of them replacing rail and the other starting the realignment of a curve. Pacific might be neglecting Midland's rolling stock but they were taking remarkably good care of track which they must be on the point of losing.

When he went back to his seat he knew that Elias Bostwick and the other Midland officials had missed something important. They were planning to take over the Machete branch within a matter of weeks, extending the line westward through Devil's Canyon to tap the new silver strikes at Placer Creek. They had thought the lease-breaking suit would be a mere formality. Now it seemed obvious that Pacific wasn't planning it that way at all.

The conductor came through the car and Quincy stopped him, asking a question intended to be merely an entering wedge for a more intelligent query. "Is this a new line, sir?"

The trainman seemed undecided whether to be amused or annoyed. He let a twisted grin show briefly under his shaggy mustache, and glanced nervously around the car. "No use playin' games, Mr. Quincy," he said. "I can't tell you nothin' and it'll be easier fer me if I don't have to talk to you." Then he was hurrying on back to the rear.

Quincy's first impulse was to swear. All of this ridiculous play-acting had been useless; it hadn't fooled anybody, Then he forced himself to think of more important angles. For one thing it was clear that Midland's plans were known to Pacific. The deal between himself and Elias Bostwick had been supposedly a deep secret—but Pacific knew about it. So they must know what Midland proposed to do about extending the Machete line up through Devil's Canyon. The fact that Pacific crews were improving Midland track reinforced his suspicion that Pacific didn't expect to lose the leased line. They were working on it because they expected to keep it and to extend it through the canyon. Somewhere Bostwick had missed an important point.

Now Quincy's annoyance was deeper. It had been bad enough to feel that people were laughing at his appearance. It was worse to think that they were laughing at his predicament. Probably every man in the car knew that he was going nowhere to do nothing. He couldn't blame them for being amused.

Partly as a matter of defiance he looked around him, suddenly knowing that he still hadn't got it right. These men in the day coach were not amused. They were watching him, all right, but it was a sullen watchfulness, a hostility which left him perplexed. Then he remembered the conductor's uneasy attitude. It made him feel a little better. If people feared or resented his arrival it must be because his situation was not as hopeless as he had feared.

He was still trying to work out the puzzle when the train reached Machete. From the car window he could see a decent-looking little town sprawled out in the curve of a hill. Having studied the map carefully he knew that he was looking at an odd spur of the Elks, the range which blocked off the lower Boulder River valley from the higher ground to the west. From Pike Junction to Machete the rail line had been a matter of routine construction, following the easy grades along the Boulder. From Machete upstream it would be rough. Devil's Canyon was the only passage through the towering Elks—and Devil's Canyon was reputed to be a tough nut to crack.

The train grated to a shuddering halt at a depot that was mostly a telegraph shanty, a baggage shed, and a cinder platform. Passengers were crowding toward the doors of the car, evidently anxious to get out. Quincy wondered if they were like the conductor, a bit afraid to be seen in his company.

He was elaborately casual as he followed the others to the platform, looking around him as though his only interests were the bright April sunshine and the stark mountain scenery. Because he was forewarned he spotted the reception committee at once. At least he felt certain that the two men at the corner of the telegraph shack constituted such a body. They moved toward him at once, and the other passengers showed notable haste in getting out of the way. Quincy couldn't quite figure it out. The arrival of a Midland engineer in Machete didn't warrant so much planned hostility. Someone must be organizing it—and for a purpose.

He pretended not to notice, turning toward the baggage car as though interested only in claiming his luggage. Still he had managed a fast appraisal of the approaching pair. One was a man fully as tall as himself, a lank, loose-jointed individual whose lantern jaw made him look all the more angular. The other was six inches shorter and probably twenty pounds heavier, a burly bear of a man whose whiskers carried out the impression of a recent hibernation. Both wore heavy shirts instead of the jackets which the brisk spring air demanded, and Quincy thought he knew why. Coat tails might interfere with a gun hand, and both men were wearing gun belts.

His apparently casual indifference seemed to infuriate them, for he heard an angry grunt behind him as he walked along toward the forward car. Then a gruff voice behind him rasped, "Hold it right there, mister!"

He went on unheeding and was almost at the baggage-car door before they overtook him, one on each side. It was the shorter man who spoke, his voice harsher now as he looked up into Quincy's face. "I said for you to wait up!" he snapped. "Don't you hear good?"

Quincy studied him mildly, half-amused at the angry bloodshot eyes which seemed to burn through the whiskers from positions athwart a bulbous red nose. "Speaking to me?" he asked quietly. "Sorry. I was in a hurry to get my bag out of the car before the train pulls out of the station."

"You won't need no bag," the tall man broke in from the other side. "We're tellin' you now to git back aboard that car and forget that you ever wanted to come to Machete."

Quincy deliberately turned to pass a steady order to the hesitant trainman in the baggage car. "Slide her out, my friend," he directed. "These boys have made a mistake."

The baggageman shook his head but obeyed. Quincy reached for the heavy cowhide portmanteau, but as he did so he felt the clutch of the burly man on his left elbow and heard the exasperated curse of the fellow on the other side.

"Damn you, Quincy!" the lanky one snapped. "Have we got to teach you some manners?"

Quincy's reply was to seize the handle of the bag and haul it toward him, sweeping it down and around in a backhanded sweep. The bag was a heavy one and its momentum made it an effective weapon. It knocked the lanky man's legs completely out from under him and at the same time the move broke the other fellow's grip on Quincy's arm.

The thin man had already drawn a gun, but the weapon spun to the cinders as he fell. Before either man could recover, Quincy dropped his bag and picked up the .45, held it on the human grizzly.

"Get your hand off that gun butt!" he snapped. "I don't know what in hell you tinhorn badmen think you're doing but it's all over. Turn around, squatty! You on the ground, stay where you are and don't make a move!" He raised the gun an inch or two as he spoke.

Quincy knew that he had an open-mouthed audience on the depot platform but he kept his attention on the immediate enemy, disarming the burly man and then stepping back so that only the train was behind him. Then he snapped an order at the pair. "Git!" he said.

They went. The burly man didn't even look back but the other one threw a curse at Quincy as he scrambled to his feet and limped after his companion. They hurried across the platform, crossing the rutted patch of red clay that separated the depot from the first strip of board sidewalk which marked the town itself.

There was a long interval of flat silence while the onlookers melted away. Then the baggageman spoke from the car door.

"You won that round, Mister Quincy, but that pair ain't goin' to let you get way with it. Keep your eyes skinned for them."

Quincy turned to face him. "I'll remember. Any idea why they're so anxious to pick a fight with me?"

The trainman shrugged as though he didn't propose to commit himself. "Nobody wants Midland bustin' in, I reckon."

The train jolted forward, and Quincy was left to puzzle some more. Somebody had learned a lot about Midland's plans. Somebody had done a pretty thorough job of advertising the arrival of one John Adams Quincy. Somebody was mighty anxious to keep that same Mr. Quincy from establishing himself in Machete.

He stared down at the two revolvers in his hands, noting

that one of them had three nicks filed on its butt. Professional gun slingers. That mysterious somebody must be serious—and worried.

He saw that one of the guns was a Colt's Frontier Model, while the one with the notches was an old Prescott Navy Revolver, probably a war relic but in good working order. He dropped a weapon into each side pocket of the blue coat; it ruined the natty set of the garment but he was no longer worried about looking like a greenhorn. At least a dozen men in Machete could testify that he was not what he looked.

Carrying the heavy bag he crossed the clay plaza to the sidewalk, aware that the depot was only a small part of more extensive railroad properties. There was a warehouse up the track a short distance, and beyond it were some six or eight sidings, all of them well filled with freight cars. If Pacific was preparing to build rail into Devil's Canyon, they had plenty of material on hand.

At the first corner he spotted a brick building whose barred windows identified it as the local lockup. Adjoining it was a frame structure with a sign over its door: SHERIFF, COUNTY OF ELK.

In the office, a fat, unshaven man dozed in an armchair with his brogans on an untidy desk. A trickle of brown ran under one edge of his sandy mustache. The vest which didn't quite cover his ample paunch was wrinkled back so that it almost hid the silver star which was pinned to it.

"You the sheriff of this county?" Quincy asked without ceremony.

The fat man pulled the vest around significantly. "I'm wearin' the badge, ain't I?"

Quincy studied him for a moment. "A little action around town would convince me more than a badge," he said finally. "You seem to let hoodlums do as they please."

"You makin' a complaint?" the sheriff snapped.

"Call it that. Two men tried to jump me at the depot. Here." He pulled the guns out of his pocket and dropped them on the desk. "If anybody claims either of these things you'll know who the guilty parties were. If it'll do any good I'm making a formal complaint."

The lawman stared numbly at the guns for a moment or so, disbelief plain on his broad features. "Got their names?" he muttered after a while.

"No. And I'm beginning to think it wouldn't do any good. You can go back to sleep now."

Quincy went out without listening to the fat man's protests. He felt pretty certain that the sheriff had known all about the proposed attack upon the town's unwelcome visitor. That added to the puzzle. How did it happen that the town, citizens and officials were so willing to go along with Pacific's interest in the matter?

On the street again he looked around for a hotel and found one without trouble, a stone-fronted building only half a block away. By that time he understood that Machete was not just another mining town of slab shacks and false fronts. Most of the buildings were substantial, many of them brick or stone. Which made it all the more remarkable that the law should be mixed up in a threat of open violence.

At the hotel desk a spry-looking little man greeted him genially, and Quincy asked, "Don't you know me? I'm Quincy. It's out of fashion in this town to be civil to me."

The little man winked. It was a surprising gesture because his thin hair, rimless spectacles and lean face gave him the look of a humorless and somewhat unhealthy ascetic. "I'm kinda out of fashion myself," the little man told him. "Anyway a hotel has got to take in any critter who's got money to pay. I reckon nobody'll press me none."

"You mean there's been pressure to make people hostile to me?"

"Sure. I figured you'd find it out before this. Didn't Ames and Winters meet you at the depot?"

"If you mean a tall skinny gunman and a stocky man with whiskers—yes."

"Sounds like them. I take it they didn't scare you none."

"Not much," Quincy replied. "Who's stirring it up?"

"Hard to tell for sure. Mostly Ames does the talkin'. Come on; I'll take you to your room."

It was hint enough. The hotel man had been friendly but he was not going to let his mouth get him into trouble. Quincy decided not to press it. He might need information worse a little later.

Alone in his room he slipped out of his fancy garments and donned his usual working garb, only omitting the heavy boots. He gave himself a few minutes for careful and uninterrupted thought and then he went out into the street again. With a good hour still remaining of the morning there was a good chance that he might learn a little more about this peculiar mess into which he had thrust himself.

Chapter 2

QUINCY KNEW that people were staring at him as he went on up the street but he didn't care, now that he knew why they were staring. Two blocks past the county buildings he entered a small brick structure whose gilded window letters marked it the BANK OF MACHETE. There was a bigger bank at the next corner but on this point Quincy's instructions were exact. Rocky Mountain Pacific controlled the big bank, but the smaller one was operated by an old crony of Elias Bostwick, the new president of Colorado Midland.

The place was empty of customers so Quincy addressed himself to a man who was as short as the hotel keeper and even thinner. "Mr. Thomas Pettigrew?"

The little man looked up with a sour frown that seemed to be a permanent part of the sharp features. He was in his sixties, Quincy guessed, a pair of alert blue eyes almost startling among the wrinkles. The only neat thing about his appearance was the wisp of gray hair which had been plastered across his bald spot. "I'm Pettigrew," he announced, his voice surprisingly deep. "I suppose you are John Adams Quincy. Bostwick wrote me you were comin'."

The twang in his voice made Quincy chuckle. "Vermont?" he asked.

Pettigrew frowned a little more heavily. "Elias tell you?"

"No. I've heard Vermonters before. And you might drop the full name. I don't like the fancy part even when I'm dressed for the act. I'm Jack Quincy to my friends."

"Then you'd better go back to where you'll find some of 'em," Pettigrew snapped. "You won't find none out here."

"Maybe I'd like to try."

"The more fool you if you do."

Quincy shook his head. "No use, Mr. Pettigrew. Bigger men than you have already tried to chase me away. You'll do Mr. Bostwick a lot better service if you skip the gloomy advice and tell me why this town is so set against me."

"Sit down." The little man seemed sourly resigned to his task. "I had a feeling from Bostwick's letter that he didn't know what he was getting you into. Maybe you'll take the advice when I tell you."

Quincy went to the desk instead of taking the indicated chair. "Here's the Colorado Midland Railroad's bank draft for fifty thousand dollars. I want to deposit it with you for checking purposes."

Pettigrew stared at the slip of paper Quincy had thrust at him. Then he went over to his books and made the necessary entries, saying nothing except to ask the routine questions incidental to opening an account.

Finally he came back to the desk, fixing those keen old eyes on Quincy and almost smiling. "I suppose that was to show me you're fixing to stay?"

"You can take it that way."

"Fair enough. Now how much do you know about what happened out here in Seventy-two?"

"Not much. I was building a line for the Pennsylvania at the time and I don't think I'd ever heard of either railroad involved in this fight."

"But you know that Midland lost and had to lease part of its line to Pacific?"

"Sure. I also know that they have excellent grounds for asking the courts to set aside that lease. When the decision is rendered Midland will be free to build on through Devil's Canyon and tap the silver diggings."

"Know how Midland got its present line up here from Pike Junction?"

"The usual way, I suppose, with government land grants."

"Right. Ten-square-mile blocks on both sides of the right of way. Worthless land until the railroad makes it valuable. Then the company can sell to settlers and get back some of their construction expense."

"Anything wrong with that?" Quincy asked. "The railroads create the value. Why shouldn't they get some of it?"

"Nothing wrong with the scheme. It's just the way Midland and a few other lines played it. Midland's directors picked out likely spots for towns, centers of mining country or river crossings or mountain passes. They bought that land for themselves and held it. Then they ran their rail so as to by-pass any towns that were already established. Mostly it made folks move to the important spots along the track—and the directors made a pile of money by selling town lots. It wasn't illegal but it sure made a gang of enemies for the railroads."

"You mean it happened here?"

"With an extra crooked game added. Midland built into this valley from Pike Junction because they knew there was coal, silver and some marble here. Machete was the only town worth mentioning so the folks here went whole-hog for the idea of havin' a railroad, building like mad because they figured to become a city. Then Midland stopped construction about ten miles down the valley and started to promote their own town on land owned by the directors. Everything could be hauled to that point almost as easy as it could be brought here so it looked like Machete was going to be a ghost town."

"It looks lively enough to me," Quincy objected.

"No thanks to Midland. Some of us floated a bond issue, going into debt up to our necks to get the money. Then we made a deal with Midland, paying the full cost of construction plus a bonus in return for their agreement to extend the line to Machete."

"I still don't see why you have any cause for complaint. You got what you paid for, didn't you? The track is here and the town looks prosperous."

"But Midland didn't build the track. That came after Pacific took over the lease. Midland swindled us—and stayed on the side of the law. They discovered that the speculators who laid out the town in the first place had filed some mighty optimistic plats, extending town limits almost three miles down the river. Midland built to that line and quit, claiming they had carried out their promise. They built *to* the town as it appeared on the plats but they never built *into* it. The courts upheld them."

"I begin to see your viewpoint—but you know Elias Bostwick. With him at the head of the company there won't be any more of that kind of dealing."

Pettigrew nodded. "Elias is as honest as any Wall

Streeter can be. I know it, but the town doesn't. They're still sore."

Somehow Quincy couldn't make himself feel that this was the whole explanation. Midland's crooked work had been carried on nearly three years earlier. People might remember a grudge, but there was something a lot more personal in the picture than this business Pettigrew had outlined.

"But how does the town figure to accept this lease-breaking? Pacific is bound to lose, you know. They've cheated on rates all along the line, deliberately trying to hurt Midland towns, and they've let Midland equipment go to rack and ruin. They're playing just as crooked a game as the old Midland gang did. The courts are sure to order the lease set aside."

"Likely," Pettigrew conceded. "So where do we stand then? Midland owns the track from Machete to Pike Junction. Pacific still owns everything in Machete. Pacific also owns the new track they're buildin' west into Devil's Canyon."

"They're building already?"

"Sure. Midland wasn't the only outfit to see that a line through the gulch was the only decent way to reach Placer Creek. Pacific started to build a fortnight ago."

"But why? We'll have them cut off when the lease is set aside."

"They can build more line down the valley. Plenty of room there. But Midland can't run a competing line through Devil's Canyon. It's too narrow."

Quincy didn't comment. He was beginning to get the picture with grim clarity. Midland's recovery of the valley line would not be of much use if Pacific held the gorge through the Elks. Pacific would have to build new track to the east or pay for use of the rails they now had under lease. It was beginning to look like a stalemate all around.

"Get it, do you?" Pettigrew chuckled dryly. "Pacific gets the important piece of track and Midland is left with the old line. My guess is that Pacific will have the biggest weapon for bargaining."

"You say it's impossible to run two lines through the canyon?"

"See for yourself. I reckon Pacific will be real happy to let you take a look."

Quincy stood up. "I'll do just that," he said.

The midday sun was trying vainly to bring warmth to the bare ramparts of the Elks when Quincy strode across toward a restaurant which caught his eye. The bleak mountains caught his attention, and he took time to consider Machete's geography a little more carefully.

To the north an angle of the range stuck out into the flatter country east of the range and north of Boulder valley. The mountain chain itself ran north and south for an almost unbroken three hundred miles, its slopes beginning immediately west of Machete. The town nestled in a rugged angle of the Elks but it derived its importance from its situation at the mouth of Devil's Canyon, the only break offering passage for a rail line through the Elks. Quincy couldn't see anything that looked like such an opening but he knew it was there. Its presence was the reason for all of this confusion.

The restaurant proved to be clean and well kept, and the food it served was excellent, although the sharp-nosed waitress indicated that she knew who he was and didn't particularly care about waiting on him. Again he was forced to the conclusion that the ill-nature that was being shown toward him was due to something other than an old grudge against his employers. He worked at the puzzle while he dispatched a generous meal but no answer fitted his knowledge of the facts.

Back on the street he turned north toward a building whose large sign could just be read at the distance. A livery ought to be just the spot for his next move. He assumed that he would need a horse in order to take a look at Devil's Canyon.

He passed two cross-streets on which small shops seemed to be doing a decent business, finding himself then on what appeared to be the edge of town. Now he could read all of the big sign. It announced that one Gavin O'Hara was here in the business of selling farm equipment, mining tools, clothing, food supplies, arms, ammunition, hay and feed. The same O'Hara had horses, carriages and wagons for sale or rent. The name sounded vaguely familiar to Quincy but he didn't try to identify it, studying instead the rambling collection of buildings which made up the O'Hara establishment.

He turned in at a lane which ran along one side of the store and led to a corral and a stable at the rear. By the time he reached the stable yard he knew that he was not going to be greeted by Mr. O'Hara in person. The person in charge of the stable was not a mister anything. Quincy took a quick look at the red-gold hair, the turned-up nose with its early-season freckles, and decided that O'Hara had shown strange taste in his choice of hostler. The girl was in her early twenties, tall, and slender enough so that she seemed boyish in dungarees, but her work garb could not hide the fact that she was a woman—and a reasonably attractive one.

"Anybody around here to rent out a horse?" Quincy asked, touching his hat.

"It's for that very thing I'm out here," she told him, the brogue thick on her tongue. "You'll be needin' a horse for how long?" The tone of the question as well as the wariness in her gaze told him that he was still not welcome. Somehow it seemed that she was not so much hostile as doubtful but he didn't take time to figure out the difference.

"I'm planning to ride up into Devil's Canyon as far as possible," he explained. "Can I do that and return here by early evening?"

"If you don't get waylaid," she replied.

"I see that you know who I am," he commented.

She looked away. "A pony will be three dollars fer the rest of the day. Another dollar for saddle and gear. You'll want a beast with spirit, I take it?"

"I'll leave it to you."

She took a rope from its peg by the stable door and went across to the corral. Quincy watched with keen interest while she roped a big roan, handling the bronc with the skill of an experienced wrangler. She led the horse to the stable door and tied him there while she brought out a saddle and bridle. Quincy tried to help with the saddle but she shouldered him away. "It's my job," she said shortly.

He handed her the money and climbed into the saddle, old memories coming back at the feel of leather. "I'll be late in returning," he said. "Will there be someone around?"

"If there's not you can tie up the beast to the corral. He'll not be neglected over long." Again she turned away from him as though unwilling to let the conversation continue.

Quincy rode slowly away from the livery stable, out into the open country beyond the last line of houses. He was heading west but he could see the shining rails of Pacific's new track some distance away to the south, evidently following the bank of the Boulder. Around an angle of the town were the rail yards he had noticed earlier. He cut across at a slant, approaching the river and railroad through a sizeable stand of timber that masked the east end of the canyon.

Halfway through the pines he crossed a rail line. It was not very old but it was rusty and obviously neglected. He studied it for some moments, trying to understand its meaning. No one had mentioned any such spur as this. It seemed to lead from the main line just west of Machete through the timber and into the first hills of the Elks along the spur. Because he was getting tired of mysteries he was tempted to trace it out, but his better judgment warned him that it would be a foolish move. His real concern was with Devil's Canyon. That had to be his first objective.

Two hundred yards beyond the rail line he broke out of the timber to find more track ahead of him, this time bright new track on a roadbed which flanked the rushing, muddy Boulder River.

Now he could see the entrance to the canyon. What had appeared to be merely a fold in the mountain range now showed itself as a deep cleft in the granite barrier. As yet the cleft did not appear to go all the way through but his study of the maps told him that such was the case. It had already been surveyed by two different companies and both surveys indicated that it was a possible railroad cut.

He rode upstream along the new track, studying the mountains ahead of him. A handcar bearing two men passed him going down toward Machete and one of its pumping operators waved a casual hand in passing. Quincy grinned. At least he had got a reasonably friendly salute from the first men he met. Probably it wouldn't be so chummy a little later.

Ten minutes of easy riding took him around a bend of the canyon and he could see smoke rising over a shoulder of rock just ahead. Construction along this stretch had been simple enough, he realized. The grade was easy and there had been ample shoulder above the river on which to carve out a roadbed.

He recalled something Elias Bostwick had told him back in New York. There had already been one law suit over Devil's Canyon. At the time of the original surveys a federal court had ruled that both railroad companies had equal rights to use the gorge, and that neither of them could interfere with the other. To Bostwick that had meant a probable construction race, but now Quincy knew that it would not be so simple. There was something in the situation which Bostwick didn't know about, something which had to be worked out before the Midland construction problem could even be defined.

Another twenty minutes of easy riding took him around a wide bend and showed him the construction crews ahead. The sight was somehow comforting to him even though this was the camp of the enemy. As an engineer he was closing in on something he understood. After so many puzzles of other types it was good to be on familiar ground.

The character of the canyon changed rapidly beyond the big bend. It was narrower now, a real gorge cut out of the mixed stone, clay and gravel by a rushing river which seemed annoyed by the mountains' insistence on compressing it into a narrow bed. Still the construction problems had been routine, the slant of the terrain made grading easy. There would be ample room for two rail lines on either side of the stream.

There was even width enough for long sidings on which strings of work cars now lay. Pacific seemed to be working efficiently in their dash up the canyon. Plenty of material was at hand, ready for instant use as rail crews followed close on the heels of the graders. Full gangs of men were on the job and a locomotive puffed back and forth as it shoved in full cars of new materials and pulled out the strings of empties. Pacific was moving.

He rode past the work crews; no one paid any attention to him. It was noteworthy that all of the rolling stock in sight was in excellent condition, and all of it carried the name Rocky Mountain Pacific.

Presently the flat ended and the canyon cut back into its narrow confines once more. At the upper end, where the storage sidings petered out, he could see construction headquarters, an old passenger coach which had been fitted out with what looked like an over-size observation platform. Men on horseback and men afoot came and went, their haste indicating that speed was the watchword on this job. Somebody at this rolling headquarters was driving the crews hard and efficiently.

Then he spotted a familiar figure. A long, lean man swung from the car's wooden platform directly into the saddle of a horse that had been tied there. For a moment it seemed that he would come directly toward Quincy but he took one look, called out sometheng toward the car, and then whirled his mount around to the other side of the spur. Quincy had plenty of time to recognize the hatchet face and protruding jaw. Winters or Ames. He still didn't know which of the thugs was which.

Not that it mattered. The man apparently had been reporting to Pacific construction headquarters. That ought to mean something. Hostility to Jack Quincy was not simply a matter of community anger against Midland. Somebody in the Pacific organization was pushing things along. But why? Pacific seemed to have every advantage. Why should they be concerned about a Midland engineer who practically had his hands tied?

Then he pulled up beside the extension platform on the car and some of the answer suggested itself. The lone occupant of the control post was completely—but not happily —familiar.

Chapter 3

QUINCY HAD seen Jefferson Kell in the gray of West Point, the blue of the Union Army, and the rough fatigues of an engineering officer working in the van of a campaigning army. Now he saw him in a broad-brimmed hat and the fringed buckskin jacket of the frontiersman, but it was the same old Jeff Kell, very cocky and a trifle supercilious. Jeff had always been a great one to dramatize himself, especially in his dress, and now he seemed to think that high boots, fringed jacket and other accouterments made him look the big man out to conquer the wilderness.

The thought was not generous nor even fair, Quincy told himself. Jeff might have been a bit on the shallow side in the old days but now he seemed to know what he was doing. Certainly this job was going well. Maybe he had learned to be dramatic and efficient at the same time. The evidence at hand said that such was the case. Kell had already seized the initiative. He was building fast up the gorge and he had clearly been responsible for the attempt to turn Quincy back. That part was easily understood now.

Quincy pulled up at a little distance from the observation platform, fixing it so that he would not have to look up at his old rival. Jeff set great store by such trifles and Quincy didn't propose to indulge him.

"Afternoon, Jeff," he called, just loudly enough to be heard above the puffing of the approaching yard engine. "I decided not to take the warning your bully boys brought."

Kell turned to face him, pretending surprise although it seemed certain that the lanky gunman had warned him of Quincy's approach. "Howdy, Jack," he replied calmly. "Come up and have a seat. We don't mind letting you see what we're doing."

He was almost as tall as Quincy, slender, and just blond enough to seem more youthful than his thirty-three years. His suave manner completed the picture of a friendly, harmless young dude; he might have fooled anyone except an old acquaintance like Jack Quincy.

Quincy dismounted and climbed to the platform, trying to interpret the meaning behind Kell's smile. At the moment Jeff was mockingly cordial as though happy to gloat over an already defeated opponent. Quincy had a hunch that the mockery was as false as the smile. Still he couldn't make out what kind of game Kell was really playing.

His host didn't carry his act far enough to include a handshake. He merely nodded toward a deck chair and asked, "How's Midland's new chief engineer? Should I congratulate you or sympathize? They sure stuck you with a rough one."

"And gave me a tough opponent," Quincy added. "I didn't know you were handling this chore for Pacific."

"Discouraged?" Kell half-sneered.

"Not too much."

"Have you looked around the bend? Up there beyond
Rock Corner?" He pointed upstream to a spot where the
canyon bent sharply around an almost vertical wall of rock.

"I'm impressed," Quincy told him. "Is that the narrow
part I've been hearing about?"

"No. That corner's easy. Plenty of dynamite and we
break through—but up there in the place they call the
Keyhole it's really narrow."

"Still going in for lots of powder, eh?" Quincy remarked
dryly.

Kell did not turn, pretending to be absorbed in the work
of a drilling crew that was preparing to blast a ledge of rock
about four hundred yards up the gorge, but the color came
into his face and Quincy thought he could see his jaw
muscles tighten. Jeff Kell had made mistakes before on the
subject of explosives. Twice he had almost tied up General
Grant's final campaign by overindulgence in blasting, cutting out bridge supports instead of merely preparing rocky
ground for them.

Neither man spoke for several minutes, then Quincy
decided to resume the offensive. If it suited Kell to pretend
casual friendliness then it ought to be a good move to play
it some other way. No point in letting the game run on the
way Kell wanted it to go.

"You think this Keyhole place is too narrow for two
tracks, is that it?"

Kell laughed shortly. "It's going to be a hell of a job
laying one line of rail through there. A second line is out
of the question."

"So I'm licked before I start?"

"Of course."

"Then why did you have those thugs of yours try to jump
me in Machete this morning? It isn't reasonable to go out
of your way to discourage an opponent who's already
licked."

Kell's eyes were angry as he swung to face Quincy. "Who
says I sent anybody to do anything?"

"I do. One of your brave lads was reporting here when
I rode up. Nobody else has any reason to rawhide me the
way I've been getting it from the folks in Machete. I don't
doubt for a moment that you've been teaching folks to hate
me ahead of time. Why?"

"Still think you're a real smart character, don't you?" Kell sneered. "Well, don't start accusing where you can't prove. This isn't the army now. This time you don't have a couple of softheaded friends up the ladder to play your game for you. I'm running things around here—and I'm going to see that it stays that way."

A quiet voice interrupted at Quincy's elbow. "No temper, Jeff," the voice cautioned. It was the voice of a woman, well restrained and oddly familiar.

Quincy turned to see that a small, dark-haired woman of about his own age had come to the door of the coach. He had been astonished to find Jeff Kell running the show for Pacific but now his amazement was so great that he couldn't find words. His thoughts wanted to turn back a dozen years but he knew that he had to keep his wits.

"Surprised to see me, Jack?" she asked, her tone calm and pleasant.

"You could knock me over with the proverbial feather," he replied after a brief hesitation. "What in the world are you doing in a construction car?"

"Helping—I think. I presume you didn't know that I'm Elinor Kell now."

He knew he should have expected that but he was still numb from the surprise of seeing her. "Lucky Jeff," he managed to say. "The last thing I heard about you was while the war was still going on. You were supposed to be marrying someone else."

"My first husband died a little over two years ago. I met Jeff and it seemed pretty fine to recall old times. We married. It was as simple as that."

He could sense that she was trying hard to make it sound casual. His thoughts went back to that last year at West Point, a hectic year when the authorities at the Academy were rushing cadets through to commissions in order to fill the gaps in the federal armies, gaps made by the desperate fighting of Confederate troops who had lost the war but would not admit it. In spite of the pressure of the times there had still been time for the inevitable romances of youth and Elinor Markham had been courted by both Quincy and Kell. The rivalry had been bitter but, as usual in the feuds between the two cadets, Quincy had won. Elinor had promised to marry him.

"Funny how things turn out," he heard himself saying.

"Hold your ears," Kell interrupted. "They signaled for the blast."

- The interruption permitted Quincy to regain his composure and he watched silently while the crew up the canyon scattered for cover. The blast came a second later, sending a geyser of rock ledge into the air.

The ensuing concussion rattled the car and beat against the faces of the watchers. No one spoke until some of the dust and rubble began to settle back into the gorge. Then Elinor spoke sharply. "Who ordered that charge?"

"I did. Naturally," her husband retorted, anger clear in his voice.

"I wish you'd leave it to O'Connell. He knows dynamite. He'd never have used so much. Now we'll have the chore of cleaning up a lot of rock that never should have been shattered."

Quincy began to understand a lot of things. It didn't make sense but he knew he was right about it. Kell was not running this job; Elinor was! And Kell had not liked the idea of having an old rival appear on the scene to spot the truth of the situation.

Jeff made no answer to his wife's complaint, and presently she went to the side of the platform and motioned to someone along the track. Then she announced crisply, "I'll ride up there and see how big a mess you've made. Quincy, you might as well ride along with me. Just beyond the second bend you can take a look at the upper gorge and see why it's hopeless for you to think of running an extra line through here."

Quincy smothered his grin. She was being very much the manager now, trying to impress him even as she seemed to have done with Jeff Kell. He merely nodded, content to watch Jeff seethe.

He maintained his silence while a workman brought a pony that had been rigged up with a fine lady's saddle. Then he stepped down to the ground, helping her from the platform and into the saddle. It was hard to remember her new status when he had her so close. The eleven-year interval had left few marks upon her and he realized that she was still a very pretty woman. Her figure was still as trim as in the days when she was belle of Academy social affairs and her hair was the same gleaming chestnut that he remembered from the past. Not a wrinkle marred the perfection of her complexion and her eyes still were the most notable feature in a piquant oval face. It did not seem possible that this girl had just been making noises like a construction boss.

He said as much as he reined his horse along beside hers, ignoring the glare which he knew Kell was aiming at his back. They were some distance up the gorge as he concluded, "It's pretty hard to remember that it's been eleven years since we parted."

"Since you deserted me," she corrected, looking straight ahead.

"Deserted? You know better than that. I told you then why we shouldn't marry. I simply had a hunch that I wasn't going to survive the war and I didn't feel that it was fair to risk making you a widow at the age of nineteen. I was pretty hurt that you wouldn't see my side of it."

She nodded, still avoiding any side glance at him. "Now I know that you were honest about it. But at the time I thought you were looking for an excuse to get rid of me. I thought you had fallen in love with someone else and I was terribly angry. That's why I told you I never wanted to see you again."

"We were both pretty silly," he murmured. "I was mighty set on my hunch about being killed. Read too many war stories, I suppose. As it turned out I spent the last few months of the war in one of Colonel Haupt's construction battalions, trying to keep supply railroads built behind Grant's army. Except for a couple of brushes with old Jubal Early's cavalry I never saw any combat."

"I know about that," she reminded him. "Jeff was in the same regiment. His stories make it clear that you had no other girl—but I didn't know it then. You never wrote so I never tried to find out about you."

"I didn't write because I took you at your word when you told me that you never wanted to see or hear from me again."

"Very childish, both of us," she said. "And what a pity."

"You seem to have done very well," he pointed out dryly.

She made no comment until they had let their horses pick a way through the rubble left by the dynamite blast. It had been too big a charge, Quincy saw. There was going to be a lot of fill necessary before grading for rails could

start. He caught a sign between Elinor and a red-faced
foreman and knew that they were thinking the same thing.

They continued in silence along a rough path which
wound along the river bank beyond the site of the blast.
He could see up the canyon for a distance of perhaps two
miles now and there was nothing in view that looked like a
real construction problem. On both sides of the tumbling
Boulder the banks sloped back at a fairly easy angle, only
going up into cliffs at some distance from the stream.

"Where is this place they call the Keyhole?" he asked
finally.

She pointed ahead. "See where that tall piece of rock
seems to block off the canyon?"

"Sure."

"That's another bend. Rock Corner, the men call it.
Beyond that corner there's another easy strip of maybe
a half mile or more. Then the canyon becomes something
utterly fantastic. They tell me that the town got its name
because it was the entrance to what used to be called
Machete Gulch. Someone with imagination thought that
the break in the main ridge of the Elks looked as though
it had been sliced out with a machete. Later a superstition
arose that the place was haunted. So it became Devil's
Canyon. Either name is good enough—and suitable."

They rode on again in silence, neither of them willing
to start a new conversation. At Rock Corner she motioned
him to follow in single file, leading the way around a point
of solid rock which almost overhung the river. From the
appearance of the river bank he guessed that at one time
there had been a good shoulder all along this side of the
stream but that erosion had taken away almost everything
up to the rock itself. A moment or two later he was no
longer interested in Rock Corner. Straight ahead of him
was the Keyhole, a narrow slot of rushing water between
towering, almost perpendicular rock walls. They were still
a long distance away from the narrow part but even now
he knew that the accounts had not been exaggerated. The
Keyhole was something that would challenge any engineer.

Elinor led the way up the canyon another two hundred
yards, pulling up where there was room for the horses to
stand side by side. From that point Quincy could see that
the Keyhole was really little more than a deep fissure, as
though the main ridge of the Elks had split apart to let

Boulder River pour through. It was simply a dark abyss with sheer, rock walls a good thousand feet high on either side. At this hour of the afternoon it was almost totally dark down in the hole, only a ripple of white water catching the light rays at the mouth.

"See what we mean?" Elinor said finally.

He nodded. "Not much room for rail in there. Figure to make it a tunnel job?"

"Probably. Jeff wants to blast out a shelf along the north wall but I tell him he'll tumble down half of the cliff if he tries it. We'd have to dig out a new canyon if that rock ever began to come down."

"You seem to know quite a lot about this business," he commented. "How did you happen to become a lady engineer?"

"Through my first husband. I married him just about a year after you and I made our mistake. He was a businessman, and a smart one. He made money on war materials and invested it in railroads because he realized that there would be a railroad-building boom once the war was over. Because he was smart he learned all he could about the business he expected to control. I went everywhere with him and I learned a lot too."

"I can understand that. You never were stupid except when you thought I was lying to you."

"Please, Jack. It's best not to . . . well, anyway I became very much interested in railroad construction. My husband speculated with the stock of Rocky Mountain Pacific and became its biggest shareholder. It was mostly his operation that drove Colorado Midland to the wall. Just as he was about to reap the benefits of his planning he died of pneumonia. It left me as the biggest stockholder of the line and I determined to carry on in his place."

"Who made the mistake of getting careless with the Midland lease?" he asked quietly.

"My mistake," she admitted. "I left it to others because my interest was in building new lines. When I learned what was happening it was too late. The suit had already been filed. I think you must understand what my plans now include. If you don't I'll not tell you."

"I can guess. But when did Jeff come along?"

"He was hired as a construction engineer by our St. Louis office. We met and renewed our friendship. In a short time we married. Again I'll not go into details."

Quincy nodded. "We'd better be riding back," he said. "The afternoon is going pretty fast."

She swung her horse without a word, leaving him to follow around Rock Corner. Quincy felt certain that he knew what was going through her mind. She had found out too late that Jeff Kell was incompetent. Jeff had been a poor student at the Academy. Probably he would never have graduated if fate had not placed him in a wartime class when the pressure was on to turn out new officers for the army. In Haupt's regiment he had been such a notable failure that at the close of the war he had been kept away from real engineering projects. Now he was trying to act like the boss of a big job—and not fooling anyone who knew the business. It was no wonder that his wife was unwilling to discuss the matter.

It had been a disturbing afternoon all around, Quincy thought. He had learned the answers to some of his questions but they were answers that satisfied little except personal curiosity. He understood what the opposition was planning to do and he could estimate how efficiently they would go about it but he had not gained anything of importance. His own problem was now stark and clear in his mind. All he had to do was remember the look of that black canyon. His problem was the Keyhole. But where was the key?

Chapter 4

THE AFTERNOON was waning fast when they approached the headquarters car, neither of them had spoken a dozen words on the return trip. It was Elinor who broke the silence, her short laugh not quite ringing true.

"Quite a reunion we've had, Jack. I wonder what either of us would have thought a dozen years ago if anyone had predicted that such an occasion might lie in the future?"

"Twelve years?" Quincy repeated. "To me it would have sounded fantastic only twelve hours ago."

Again her laugh was a trifle too brittle. "On that score I had the advantage. We heard about your coming last week. It gave me a chance to steady myself."

He shot a sidelong glance at the well-remembered profile. "Then this meeting meant something to you?"

"Of course. There's no reason for us to play cute about it, Jack. We're long past that stage. I once loved you very much, perhaps more than I've loved either of the men I married. A woman doesn't get over that kind of love so easily."

He nodded, not looking toward her. "I appreciate your telling me that, even if it can't be much consolation. Maybe it helps me to recognize that my recent career as a woman-hater has been pretty much of a sham. I've just been hating to cover up the hurting."

There was a long pause before she said, "I hope you won't be hurt any more by what is going on here now. Our past must remain the past but there's no reason to let the rest of the situation cause you added trouble. Get out while you're still clear."

When he made no reply she added quickly, "That's honest advice, Jack. I gather from what you said a while ago that there was another attempt to warn you off but this time the warning is an honest one. You'll be butting your head against a stone wall here."

"My employers didn't seem to think so."

"Your employers are a long way from Devil's Canyon. I don't think they even suspect what you must be realizing by this time. We know that we can't win that lease suit but we are certain that we can delay the decision. We've got the best attorneys in the country working for that delay. By the time Colorado Midland regains control of the track between Pike Junction and the former railhead east of Machete we'll have our rail through Devil's Canyon. You can see what that will mean, I'm sure."

"It's pretty clear. We'll have one rail line from Pike Junction through the canyon, about half of it owned by each company."

She shook her head. "You understand it better than that, Jack. Midland will own about forty miles of track which will be useless. With a little time and expense we can duplicate it if Midland won't sell it to us. On the other hand we'll own track which can't be duplicated. We'll be able to dictate terms and Midland won't be able to do a thing about it."

Again he was silent, knowing that there was no answer to her analysis. She went on swiftly, a tone almost of pleading in her voice. "Don't be foolish enough to risk your reputation in a hopeless cause, Jack. I don't want to see you hurt. If you stay you'll have to shoulder part of the blame for failure. If you go back now and tell Elias Bostwick that you won't accept an impossible assignment no one can blame you. You'll only be doing your duty as a good engineer trying to save his company needless expense."

He could not doubt her sincerity. This was no bluff to drive him away; the woman he had once wanted to marry was simply showing concern for his welfare. It suddenly occurred to him that he now had the answer to all of the morning's questions. He knew why Pacific was taking good care of Midland track while they neglected Midland rolling stock. He knew why Pacific was running in so much construction material. He even knew why thugs had been sent to drive him away.

She seemed to read his mind. "There's a selfish reason behind that warning, of course," she admitted. "It's the same reason that caused Jeff to send those men. He couldn't stand the thought of having you know how this job is being run. It's no easier for me . . . but I'm married to him and I propose to make the best of it. Among strangers we can hope to keep it our secret that Jeff has to be watched so carefully. With you around . . ." She let her voice trail off as though realizing that she did not need to spell it out any more definitely.

It was the answer to his third question but it was certainly the most unsatisfactory answer of all. For a while he had thought he was on the trail of a weakness in Pacific's position. The attempt to scare him off had sounded like an admission of vulnerability. Now the real reason was plain—and the Pacific fortress remained impregnable.

They were close to the observation platform by that time. Kell did not appear to greet them but Quincy still kept his voice low as he said, "I'll try not to embarrass anyone." Then in a more normal voice he added, "Thanks for the tour. The company was nice even if the view was depressing."

Dusk was closing down on the mouth of the gorge when Quincy pulled his mount away from the rail line and headed into the pines. The rumble of a train behind him told him that the work crews were coming out, so he halted at the edge of the timber, curious to watch the movement.

Kell's traveling headquarters was at the rear of a string of flatcars, each of which bore its share of workmen. On the morrow there would be other cars going back to replace these empties, cars loaded with ties, rails and other material for pushing Pacific track up into Devil's Canyon. It was a depressing sight for a man who had just learned that he could not hope to compete.

He let the horse plod slowly through the pines, paying little attention to his path until he realized that he was back at the edge of town. Then he realized that he could not spot the livery stable in the darkness. Not that he cared too much. The events of the afternoon had left him in no mood to care very much about anything.

When he finally located the stable there was no one about, so he tied the horse to a corral post and started through the alley which led to the street. He was at the corner of the owner's living quarters when a rectangle of yellow suddenly appeared, a woman's silhouette appearing briefly before the light was shut out. It was an interesting silhouette and Quincy decided that the O'Hara establishment must afford more than one female. This one certainly was not the lady hostler. Then a voice inquired softly, "Would you be returning the beast, Leftenint?"

For a moment he didn't realize the significance of the query. His mind struggled with the surprise at realization that this was the same girl he had seen in the afternoon. Only as an afterthought did he realize what she had actually said.

"I tied the horse at the corral," he stammered. "Are you . . . Wait! You called me Leftenint! Only one person ever spoke it like that—and his name was O'Hara."

"Will you be quiet?" she hissed. "It's not smart business in this man's town to be getting friendly with the likes of you."

He moved closer to her in the darkness, his voice dropping to a whisper that would match hers. "The name on your sign is Gavin O'Hara. Sergeant Gavin O'Hara, formerly of the Union Army, always called me Leftenint. What goes on here?"

"He wants to talk to you—on the quiet. You'll slip in quickly."

"You forgot your brogue," he chuckled, smiling to himself. "What kind of game are you playing here?"

The girl laughed softly but with good humor. "It's easy to forget when one has an Irish father and a German mother. I like to play games, as you call it. Any objection?"

"None. What's this about it being bad business to deal with me?"

"Just that. Sheriff Naylor and his crowd run this town in their own way. Naylor passed the word that you were not to be helped. People who expect to stay in business here generally go along with Naylor's orders. Ready now? Slip in when I open the door."

She practically pushed him into what was obviously the O'Hara kitchen, giving him no opportunity to ask further questions about Machete's political boss. There was a plump, blond woman working at the stove, an appetizing odor attesting to the excellence of her cooking. No one else was in the room. The girl had not followed him.

"Mrs. O'Hara?" he asked, taking off his hat.

"Ja," she replied with a warm smile. "Sit down, please. My husband come pretty soon." She seemed pretty casual about it.

He took a seat near a window with close-drawn curtains. The blond woman said something which he could not understand, most of it being in German or heavily accented English. Memory began to come back and he recalled that Sergeant Gavin O'Hara, the best supply man in Haupt's regiment, had been married to a German girl he had met coming over on the boat from the old country. O'Hara had spoken often of his "Dutch wife" and of the little girl he had left behind when he entered the army.

Eleven years since demobilization! It didn't seem possible. O'Hara's "little girl" had probably been born in the early 'fifties. That would make her about twenty-three or four now. The lady hostler must be that same little girl. He recalled the silhouette in the doorway and amended his estimate. Miss O'Hara was no longer just a little girl.

Before he could work on the idea there was an interruption. A burly man whose graying hair contrasted sharply with a flowing red mustache came into the kitchen, a grin spreading over square-cut features at sight of the visitor. He rushed across to take the engineer's hand in a big paw but his voice was a cautious whisper as he greeted, "Real glad to see you, Leftenint! The lass told you about everything, I reckon?"

"In her own way," Quincy assured him with a small grin. "We have to meet on the sly because it's not good business for O'Hara to act decent to a Midland man."

The bushy brows pulled down into a troubled frown. "It don't sound good when you put it like that, Leftenint. Not that it ain't true, you'll understand."

"I don't blame you. Was it Kell who passed the word to boycott me?"

"You know about Kell then?"

"Sure. I made a sort of social call on him this afternoon."

O'Hara looked surprised. "Kinda prompt, wasn't you? Seems to me yourself and the leftenint wasn't real good friends in the old days."

"We weren't—and we're not. I just happened to run across him. It was a real surprise to find him in charge of Pacific construction."

"No more'n it was to me when he showed up here. In the army we had to pull him out of plenty holes of his own making. I can't figure how the man holds his job without there being somebody back of him to keep him straight."

"You've met him since he arrived?"

"In passing. But I never let on. He don't know I ever had a thing to do with him. Did he admit he stirred up talk against you?"

"Practically. I suppose he didn't want an old rival like myself to see how much of a fraud he still is. He wanted to drive me off before I could understand a few things about him."

"Maybe there's another reason," O'Hara began. "I been thinking——"

This time the interruption was at the outside door. It opened swiftly and a tall girl in a plain but well-fitted gray dress came in. For Quincy it was easier to identify her as the girl of the silhouette than as the lady hostler. In the lamplight the red tint in her gold hair was a little more pronounced than it had been in daylight and she had taken some pains with it. He could still make out the pale freckles across her slightly tilted nose but there was nothing else about her to remind him of the lady roper of the corral. She was completely feminine, and very pretty.

"I took care of the horse," she reported, making no attempt to put on the brogue. "Also I think Mister Quincy was not followed. It'll be safe to have him around for a while." Her brief smile in his direction took any possible sting out of the phrasing.

" 'Tis my daughter Peggy, in case you haven't guessed," O'Hara said. "I take it you've already caught yourself a mess of Dutch gab from my wife Gretchen."

Mrs. O'Hara smiled pleasantly as she went about the business of putting food on the table, evidently content to be the target of her husband's humor. It was quite a family, Quincy decided. An Irish immigrant who had given four years of service to his adopted country and had still found time to become a reasonably prosperous business man. A wife who must have helped to build up that business but who had failed to learn much English in twenty years. A daughter who seemed to have a variety of odd talents in addition to a very notable charm. Definitely quite a family.

Suddenly Quincy realized that he had relaxed—for the first time in days. He permitted himself to be seated at a table that was well spread with a variety of dishes and for the next twenty minutes he let his problems fall away. He talked a little about the construction jobs he had handled since leaving the army but mostly he listened to the story of the O'Hara family.

Gavin had picked up a job with the Union Pacific as construction foreman as soon as he was mustered out, bringing his wife and twelve-year-old daughter with him as the track crews started their long drive across the prairies. Within a month all three of them were working, Mrs. O'Hara and Peggy running a camp commissary. The Irish track gang had liked German cooking so well that when the job was done and they had transferred as a crew to another line the O'Hara establishment had gone along with them, operating now as a private venture. By that time Peggy was sixteen and was practically bossing the job.

Their traveling restaurant had eventually found itself on

a Colorado Midland job and had been left stranded when
Midland's original company went broke and leased their
rail to Pacific. They risked their savings to set up a restaurant in Machete and the enterprise had grown into the
present general supply business. O'Hara still claimed to be
dazed by the whole development, insisting that his daughter
had engineered the whole thing.

"You'd never know she was a mixture of bull-headed
Irish and thick-headed Dutch," he told Quincy with a
broad smile. "If I hadn't raised her from a pup I'd think
we'd picked up the halfbreed brat of a Yankee and a
Scotsman."

Miss O'Hara wrinkled her nose at Quincy. "Only the
compliment of a doting father could be phrased so daintily.
I hope Mister Quincy won't think that I'm quite the schem-
er I'm made to sound."

"Mebbe he'll like your scheming when he hears what
you've got to tell him," O'Hara stated. "Git on with it. I
didn't get a chance to say a thing about it."

She became serious at once. Turning directly to Quincy
she asked, "Do you have any idea why they're trying to
scare you out of town?"

He frowned in some surprise. "We spoke of it briefly
before you came in. It seems to be a personal matter between Jeff Kell and myself."

"No more than that?" She seemed surprised and disappointed.

"What else?"

"I don't know. Maybe I've been guessing too wildly. We
had about decided that they didn't want you to see that
there might be a way of beating them to Devil's Canyon."

"How?" He almost shouted the word. "I had a suspicion
along that line but then it seemed impossible and I figured
that it was something else. If there's a chance I want to
know about it."

"Maybe it's not a real chance so don't get your hopes up.
The key to everything is Devil's Canyon, isn't it? The folks
who lay rail through the Keyhole can dictate terms."

He nodded, recalling that Elinor had used almost those
very words. "Go on. How can I manage it? By working in
from the opposite end? If so how can I get materials across
the mountains?"

"That part we can manage. The big question is whether

my idea is practical. How much time would you need in order to beat the Pacific people to the Keyhole?"

He thought it over for a moment. "They'll need nearly a week to reach Rock Corner. That will take some blasting, maybe a matter of three days or so. Call it two days more to reach the narrows. Perhaps twelve days in all. But I'm not even sure I can lay rail through the Keyhole. I haven't had a close look at it."

A heavy pounding somewhere in the front of the building cut off what she was about to say. Gavin O'Hara started toward the door which Quincy understood must lead to the store. "If the coast is clear let him out!" he snapped.

The girl nodded and went to the back door. She was gone into the night for a few seconds, returning to beckon hastily. Quincy went. He was consumed with excited curiosity but he knew that these people were the only ones who seemed to be offering him any hope of success. He had to go along with whatever program would protect them in what they were doing.

He paused in the darkness of the O'Hara back yard, letting his eyes accustom themselves to the darkness. Margaret took his arm, leading him toward the corral. "We're clear, I'm sure, but we can't risk any more talk tonight. Just before daybreak tomorrow morning go to Bud Mayhew's livery and hire a horse. No more business here for the time being. Ride straight out past Mayhew's and in about a half mile you'll cut an old wagon trace that leads up the north mountain. I'll be ahead of you with a freight wagon. Don't try to catch up until you're at the top of the ridge. Got that clear?"

"Right. What will happen then?"

"You can take a look at something. If you want to use the idea I'll undertake to provide you with six or eight good men, a little over three miles of good used rails and ties, and whatever tools you need."

"Rails? Where . . .?"

"Maybe you saw an old siding in the pines. Father bought it for scrap when the coal company went broke. Don't take the time to ask now; just trust me on that score. Now get on your way—and don't take any chances. You made some mean enemies today."

He was halfway back to the hotel when some of the excitement drained away. The girl's enthusiasm had been so contagious that he had not let himself realize how ridiculous the whole thing was. A girl who knew nothing of construction was proposing some harebrained scheme which she didn't even dare explain. She had offered six men when he needed two hundred. She proposed to sell him some old track that would have to be torn up and transported across an impossible mountain before it could be used. And the whole project had to be carried out in no time at all while a powerful enemy was in position to thwart every effort.

He was feeling pretty glum by the time he reached the hotel, certain that he had not been tailed at any time. Still he asked about the location of Bud Mayhew's livery and made arrangements to be called a good hour before daybreak. Even a crazy scheme was better than no scheme at all.

Chapter 5

ONLY A hint of color was in the eastern sky when Quincy left the hotel next morning, still more than half asleep, unshaven and without breakfast. At that moment he would have been the first to admit that his present move was sheer folly. A pretty girl had offered him a straw to grasp and he was acting like a half-baked schoolboy.

The town was already astir, men hurrying toward the rail yards with lunch pails in their hands. It made him realize how weak his chances were. Pacific was driving hard with full crews and the best of equipment. How could he hope to beat that combination?

Still he followed Margaret O'Hara's orders. Maybe he was getting to be another Jeff Kell, depending on a woman to tell him his business. It was not a happy thought but he didn't let it stop him. A man had to play the cards that were dealt him if he had any hopes of making a lucky draw.

He found Mayhew's livery stable without difficulty, hiring a horse that looked sturdy enough even though it was not up to the standard of the O'Hara animal. No one seemed to recognize him at the stable but he kept a close watch on his back trail as he left town, aware that some of the workmen had stared at him suspiciously.

Day was breaking by the time he struck the first upgrade north of the town so he halted in a clump of piñons, waiting there for several minutes while he scanned the flat country behind him. When no one moved there he sent the horse on up the steep slope, presently striking a faint wagon trail which climbed at something of an angle into the northeast. Fresh wheel marks told him that Miss O'Hara had carried out her part of the move.

He let his horse idle along for a good half hour, stopping several times to study the slopes behind him. Even when he caught the clink of harness on the slopes above he did not hurry, remembering the girl's instructions. Thirty added minutes of climbing found him on a shoulder of the mountain and for the first time he understood the terrain completely. This odd spur of mountain which stuck out to the east from the main north-south chain of the Elks was quite a chunk of granite. It separated Machete from valley country to the north just as the big ridge cut it off from the western valley. He could only guess at the location of Devil's Canyon. He knew that it was somewhere immediately west of his present position but the folds of the mountain completely hid the narrow cut.

When he was sure that his ride had not been observed he rode on across the spur summit to a spot where the trail forked. The right-hand trace seemed to lead into the big valley north of the spur while the left fork wound along to the summit of the main range and then down into the valley of the Boulder. A glance at the wagon marks told him to take the left fork.

Twenty minutes later he saw a freight wagon ahead, its six-mule team taking a breather after the hard climb. He pulled up alongside, touching his hat to the girl on the driver's seat. Once more she was in the ragged outfit she had worn at the stable, but her hair was neat and the general impression was striking rather than careless.

"Glad you're on time," she greeted. "I'd rather no one came along to see us here."

"Of course. Now what's the plan?"

She shook her head. "I want you to find it for yourself; you're the engineer, not me. Just ride through the trees off

there to the left and when you hit an open space look for
a spire of rock that sticks up in the distance above the
trees. Head straight toward it until you reach another bare
patch. You'll find more timber beyond the second opening
but don't ride into it. Tie your horse and walk forward. Be
careful because the canyon opens out in front of you without any warning. Take a good look around and see if you
come up with an idea. If you don't . . . then mine was
no good."

He smiled at her. "Do you always play riddle games like
this?"

"I'm doing it this time."

"Suit yourself. I won't argue. What happens after I take
my look?"

"Come back to this trail. Follow my wagon tracks down
into the valley to the west. You'll see a ranch down there
just beyond the timber. It belongs to a man named Muldoon. He's part of the plan—if there is one. I'll be at his
place."

She picked up the reins with her left hand, flicking the
long rawhide whip out over the mules' backs with the
other. The coil darted and cracked explosively as she
shouted a string of syllables which Quincy could not understand. Apparently the mules understood, however, for
they leaned into their collars to start the heavy wagon into
reasonably rapid motion. Quincy kept pace with them until
Miss O'Hara waved him away, indicating his proper direction with a flick of the whip. "I swear at 'em in Gaelic,"
she called. "It's more ladylike and the mules know that
they're being properly cussed. That's all that counts. See
you later."

Quincy was chuckling aloud as he pulled his horse into
the timber. Whatever else might be said about Margaret
O'Hara she was interesting.

It occurred to him that he had taken a remarkable interest in a couple of women within the past twenty-four
hours. In the case of Elinor it was natural enough. His
confirmed—and rather sour—bachelorhood was directly
attributable to the old quarrel with her. Yesterday sight of
her had stirred old memories and some of the memories
had been pleasant ones. She looked so exactly like the girl
of bygone years that he still found it difficult to think of her
as a woman who was practically running a railroad.

With Margaret O'Hara it was different. Her businesslike air was one of the qualities which intrigued him. Her father's identity was also a subject for nostalgia and the girl was pretty enough, but there was something more, something Quincy could not quite name. He seemed to feel an idiotic impulse to smile when she was around and it certainly was not that she was entirely amusing.

He pushed ahead through the timber, finding the terrain just as she had described it. The granite spire was an easy landmark and he rode toward it along what he knew must be the summit of the spur. It occurred to him that Margaret O'Hara must be a pretty good woodsman as well as a business operator and source of ideas. She certainly seemed to know this mountain country.

He found the second bare strip easily enough, picketing his horse and moving ahead through the piñon growth afoot. One moment he was shoving through a particularly dense growth and then suddenly there was nothing but space in front of him. He halted so abruptly that he had to smile at his own jumpiness. Then he took another cautious step or two, trying to peer down into the depths.

There was a partial overhang a little to his left, so he moved toward it, finding a spot where he had an unobstructed view of the breathtaking drop. It was hard to believe that the little brown gutter down there was the wildly rushing Boulder River.

He knew that he was standing directly above the Keyhole. From above it looked even worse than from below. The opposite rim seemed to be only a stone's throw away but there was a good half mile of solid rock between him and the rim, a quarter of it down and another quarter back up again. On the near side the cliff was no nearly perpendicular that there was no point in calling it anything else. On the south side the slope could not have been more than ten degrees different. No wonder the old Mexican inhabitants thought that the gorge looked as though it had been sliced through the Elks with a machete.

He let his mind enjoy the sheer grandeur of it for a moment or two, but then his practical mind took charge and he studied the location for a hint as to what Margaret O'Hara had meant. At first he could see nothing, but then he spotted a break in the wall a short distance downstream. It was almost hidden from his view but it was there and he moved toward it with quick interest, working out to a tongue of rock which formed a corner of the rim. Now the drop was abrupt on two sides of his position, one wall leading straight down to the river while the other broke almost as abruptly down into a ragged cut that was not a canyon at all but a big gouge in the north cliff. Probably a flaw in the rock strata had caused some sort of slide, he thought. The geology of it wasn't important at the moment. The significant point was that here was a place where the solid rimrock gave way to a sort of slanting passageway.

He worked his way around the edge of the flaw, studying it with some excitement. The rock slippage had not been uniform down there. He could see several shelves formed by the ends of exposed strata and he knew that here was something to be considered swiftly. Experienced riggers could enter the lower gorge from this spot. Proper equipment installed here would even make it possible to lower such heavy equipment as rails and ties to the canyon floor. It would be tricky and dangerous but it could be done. The big problem would be to find enough rope and tackle—and enough men who knew how to work such things.

Another job for Margaret O'Hara, he thought with a quick grin. She had been right about this opening; maybe she could find men to take advantage of the situation.

He suddenly realized that the girl had been right on another count. She had referred to this place in trying to explain Jeff Kell's anxiety to keep Quincy out of the gorge area. It sounded like the proper guess. Kell knew of this slide. He had no use for it himself, and probably would not have been able to rig it properly, but he was afraid Quincy might find a way to do so. Quincy was almost flattered.

He was planning carefully as he made his way back to the wagon trail. There would be a considerable task in getting equipment to the rim. He would need men who could handle heavy block-and-tackle equipment. He would need men to lay rail once the stuff was lowered to the canyon floor. He would need graders and bridge-builders for the lower job. Most of all he had to find all of these with complete secrecy. If he couldn't seize that Keyhole stretch before Jeff Kell could push an advance crew into the canyon none of it would be any good.

His moment of excitement was pretty well covered by a

rising tide of gloominess by the time he was back on the trail once more, following the wheel marks of the O'Hara freight wagon. The lady hostler had come up with a real smart idea but he didn't see that there was much hope of making anything come of it.

Once more he rode in solitude, the trail breaking down over the shoulder of the main ridge and into a broad valley. So far as he could tell there had been almost no recent travel on this trail. Evidently the valley west of the Elks hadn't become important enough to have much contact with Machete.

After a long downgrade he broke out of the timber to find himself in a broad, rolling valley that was bare of anything but sagebrush. The wagon tracks were easy to follow although they didn't seem to be following any well-defined trail and presently he saw a cluster of unpainted shacks ahead of him. A wagon that seemed to be O'Hara's stood along the side of the largest shanty so he presumed that this would be the Muldoon ranch. He guessed that Mr. Muldoon was not exactly prosperous.

Margaret O'Hara came out of the house to meet him, her smile quizzical as she waved a casual hand to the bandylegged little man who ambled along beside her. "Meet Marty Muldoon," she said, letting the brogue have full sway. "It's himself that's the dirty landlord of this hovel. Muldoon, this is Mister John Adams Quincy. You've heard the O'Hara blather about him, I don't doubt."

Quincy slid from the saddle and shook hands with the grinning Muldoon. He saw that the squatty little fellow was older than he had first appeared, the round face and a couple of missing front teeth making him look more like a grinning urchin than a man of nearly sixty. "The girl's got more than a proper share of the O'Hara blarney," Quincy commented. "I'm Jack to my friends."

Muldoon met the handshake with a power that matched Quincy's. He was not big but there was plenty of strength in him, just as there was an abundance of ginger-colored whiskers around his chin. "A blathering female," he agreed solemnly, his voice a deep rumble in which the accent was almost obscured. "But a smart one. She tells me you want men."

Quincy studied him closely, hoping that the quick switch to business was a hint of real interest. "First I need an agent," he said. "An agent who can act for me where I can't act. Someone to hire men and materials and keep quiet about it."

Muldoon winked. "I know some idle lads around this part of the country and I got a friend name of O'Hara who's in the supply business. What would this job of agent be payin'?"

Quincy chuckled at the man's tone. "A bit better than the usual rate. What does a good man earn in this country?"

It was Miss O'Hara who offered the information. "A dollar to two dollars a day for farm laborers. Pacific is paying three to work crews. A poor homesteader like Muldoon usually doesn't earn anything."

"This side of the ridge is good for nothin' but cattle," Muldoon protested. "A man can't stock his range when he's got no capital to buy the beasts."

"Would twelve dollars a day help?" Quincy asked.

"For that much money I'd go into Machete and spit in Sheriff Naylor's eye!"

"Then you're the special agent for this job. Your first business will be finding a couple of foremen who know their jobs. I want one man who has had some experience with hoisting rigs. I want another who knows how to grade roadbed and lay rail. Ten a day for men who can handle those jobs. Five a day for good laborers. A bonus to everybody if we win out."

"How soon do you need 'em?" Muldoon asked, a gleam in his eyes.

"Right away. How many can you locate?"

"Eight or ten, most of them with experience at railroading. Old Midland men."

"No more than that?"

"Likely not. We got a few more good lads in this country, but the others done better'n me with their ranching. They'll give us a hand if we need them for short spells but they got planting season on them right now."

"Do the best you can. Now what's the tool-and-equipment prospect?"

"Look in that wagon," Miss O'Hara said calmly. "It's sheer coincidence, of course, but I made quite a mistake about what Muldoon ordered from our warehouse. After I brought them all the way out here I discovered that he didn't really order twenty shovels, a dozen picks, six sledge hammers, ten crow bars and some other assorted items. Now that he's an agent for the Midland people he might want to change his mind."

"See what I mean?" Muldoon grimaced. "Smart but awful gabby."

Quincy made a quick decision. He didn't have much choice. This pair had anticipated it and were already moving ahead. He had to trust them all the way.

"Let's spell it out so there will be no misunderstanding," he proposed soberly. "When I get back to town I'll arrange at the bank for Muldoon to have a drawing account to cover everything. He buys that old coal siding from Gavin O'Hara, letting people understand that he's buying it for someone else, someone who wants him to tear up the track and move the materials somewhere to the north. You know the country so you can dream up the details better than I could. Get a crew on the job of ripping up the track. Store rails and ties in convenient spots but don't make any move to load them until we're ready to make the big move. Then hire as many wagons or mule teams as you can get, putting everybody on the job for a mass movement that will be completely a surprise to anybody watching us."

"That part will work out," Muldoon assured him. "These homesteaders will be glad to put in a couple of days hiring out wagons. I'll likely have to pay about twenty a day for man and team."

"That's your choice to make—but get them. And don't tell them how far they're going to move the stuff until we are actually ready to load. We can't afford any leaks."

"Right you be."

"Meanwhile we ought to have a crew working up there on the rim, getting slings ready for lowering the stuff into the canyon. Have 'em keep out of sight until they actually start to install their ropes. When they move into the open we start hauling material. It has to be a fast move and a well-timed one or it won't be any good."

"Where do I come in?" Miss O'Hara asked, excitement shining in her blue eyes. "Don't nudge me aside now; I thought of it in the first place."

"You're my other special agent," he told her with a grin. "I've got to keep shady and seem helpless. That means I spend my time around Machete inviting folks to glare at me. Meanwhile you run the show. Right?"

"Don't put her on the payroll, boss," Muldoon cautioned. "She's figurin' a profit fer the O'Haras all along—and it'll be plenty."

Quincy laughed. "We'll not worry about that. As long as my agents handle their jobs they get their pay. If they make a little on the side I'll not complain. The important items are speed and secrecy. Beyond that I want both of you to use your own best judgment. If you guess wrong on anything I'll not hold it against you. Is that clear?"

"You got money to pay for all this?" Muldoon inquired cautiously.

"Midland's filthy rich. Don't worry on that score. Just get the men and start things moving."

They discussed details for another hour and by the time Quincy was ready to head back toward Machete he felt reasonably pleased with the state of affairs. Maybe it wouldn't work but at least he was making a move. Anything was better than waiting around in Machete while the opposition moved ahead with their construction program.

Chapter 6

BACK IN Machete there was no indication that anyone knew where he had been. At the livery stable and again at the hotel he passed comments which hinted that he had been studying the gorge to his complete disgust. It might not fool anyone but it was worth a try.

The little hotel proprietor was sympathetic and Quincy spent a few moments talking to him, aware that a bald man with a fancy vest was listening although making a pretense of reading an old newspaper. Because he had a hunch that the man might be a spy he made himself sound particularly unhappy, even suggesting that he might go back east and quit his job.

Then he went up to his room and spent a good hour in writing a long account of the situation to Elias Bostwick in New York. He warned Bostwick that the job would be merely a stop gap but would be expensive. If Midland didn't want him to proceed under such conditions they would have to let him know quickly. Otherwise he proposed to continue with such plans as might prove feasible. It was not a very diplomatic letter but he was not pleased with the inadequacies of the information that had been given him at headquarters so he pulled no punches.

It was not quite dusk when he sealed the letter and took it out to the post office which he had previously located. He didn't think that Kell or his local allies would venture to tamper with the United States mails.

The clatter and hiss of the returning work train was sounding from the river when he emerged from the post office to find Elinor Kell directly in his path. She was dressed fashionably in a flowing gown that had been partly covered by a light coat against the chill of the April evening. Her dark hair had been arranged just a bit too elaborately for a place like Machete and he had a quick suspicion that she had planned this meeting.

Regardless of her motives she made a most attractive picture, the impression of youth being even more striking than on the previous day. He found it difficult to remember that she was a woman of thirty, a majority stockholder in a railroad company.

He lifted his hat with grave courtesy, remarking, "Not building any railroads today?"

Her smile was a gay one. "My day off. I'm construction boss only when the mood seizes me. I have plenty of time on my hands and I'm very much interested in the work, so I'm afraid I sometimes make a nuisance of myself. Today I decided to catch up with my housekeeping."

He wondered whether she expected to deceive him with the remark. However he did not press the point. Instead he elected to play it the obvious way. "Apparently the housekeeping left you plenty of time for primping. You're fixed up mighty pretty."

"You noticed? I was afraid you might not."

"You haven't changed a bit, Elinor," he said, a little more seriously. "Yesterday I felt that you looked just as you looked eleven years ago. Today I find that you even talk the same way, pretending to be surprised at the compliments you know you're going to get."

"But I don't know any such thing. I . . ."

"The same old pretense. You're a mighty pretty woman, Elinor, but you still fish desperately for compliments. You don't need to do it, you know."

This time her smile faded. "You always were aggravating, Jack, and you haven't changed either. Even your compliments sound like an indictment."

"Sour grapes. You didn't marry me."

"It was your own fault—but let's not get into that kind of a quarrel. I came out to find you this afternoon so as to invite you to dinner. I may regret the invitation if you make speeches like that last one."

"Dinner?" he repeated in surprise. "I'm the enemy, in case you haven't heard. Word is out in Machete that folks are not supposed to have any dealings with me."

"Nonsense! Who would do a thing like that? Try to boycott you, I mean."

"I've been blaming Jeff but I can't prove it."

"But why should he?"

"I think we won't go into it now. I don't propose to argue myself out of a decent meal. What time is dinner?"

"Seven. Do you know where we live?"

"No."

"An apartment over the railroad office building. That's just across the plaza from the freight house." The smile came back again as she added, "But don't get any notions about sampling my cooking. Our Chinaman is entirely competent and I don't interfere with him."

She walked away swiftly and he stood for a long minute with his hat in his hand, perplexity mingling with the pleasure of watching her. It had been fun to spar with her but he couldn't quite make up his mind about her. He had a feeling that she was trying to make him forget the way she had acted toward Jeff on the job. He wondered why she should bother. At the same time he had a hunch that she had not known about the manner in which the town was treating him. He didn't suppose it really made any difference but he hoped he was right about it.

As he swung on his heel to go back to the hotel he almost ran into a pair of men who were coming down the street. One of them was the fat, sloppy individual he had seen in the sheriff's office and the other was a bleary-eyed old wreck who must have been in his early sixties but who could easily have passed for eighty. He was holding to the sheriff's arm for support and one whiff of him told Quincy that the bloodshot eyes had not been contracted by looking too long into the sun.

"Look where you're going, dammit!" the sheriff snapped as Quincy almost ran against him. "You're stirring up enough stink in this town without running around loco."

Quincy recovered himself quickly. "The law!" he exclaimed. "I trust you have located the gunmen who tried to hold me up yesterday?"

"I ain't tried," the lawman growled. "Too many hard cases around here fer me to locate a pair like you described."

"And you can't trace either gun?"

"Course not!"

Quincy kept his face solemn as he nodded. "Thanks for trying. I don't want to think that the local law can't cope with things. By the way, I have just been invited to dinner with the Chief Engineer of Rocky Mountain Pacific. He's my enemy, you know, so if I'm found poisoned I hope you will take the proper steps."

The older man hiccupped loudly and Quincy shoved past, enjoying the bewildered look on the sheriff's fat face. The boycotters might begin to wonder if it was noised around town that Kell was entertaining his rival engineer.

At the hotel Quincy gave the story a shove by mentioning the invitation to the hotel keeper. "I hope the sheriff didn't take me too seriously just now," he said with a short laugh. "I warned him that I might get poisoned because I was going to dinner with the Kells. He seemed mighty surprised that I'd been invited."

"Getting chummy with the sheriff, are you?" the little man asked, his smile not quite easy.

"No. I just happened to meet him on the street. The fat rascal had to get out of his chair long enough to take a drunk to the calaboose."

"Sounds like he was taking Judge Potter home. Long about this time of night he's generally doing that. Potter's the county judge of Elk."

"Nice combination. A lazy sheriff who pays no attention to the thugs who run loose and a drunken judge who ought to be in a home for alcoholics. No wonder some of you folks talk soft about such matters."

"We ain't found any way to bust it," the little man

growled, his voice cautiously low. "Don't figure Naylor as a fat slob who's just lazy. He runs this town and he's plenty tough. That act of looking lazy is part of his game. Keeping Potter drunk and under control is another part of it. Don't prod him too much or he'll find a way to hurt you bad."

"Thanks," Quincy told him. "That's the best anybody has spelled it out for me so far. I'll remember. It explains a lot of things."

He bathed and shaved with extra care, going out on the street with a good five minutes to spare before seven o'clock. It was only a couple of blocks to the office building whose second story had been turned into living quarters for the Kells, and a clock was striking the hour as he was admitted to a rather sumptuous apartment. Jeff met him at the door, his manner hinting that he hadn't approved of the invitation but that he would make an effort to be civil. Quincy took the cue and played it the same way.

The dinner was an excellent one and the table conversation remained impersonal as both men refused to play up to Elinor's attempts at gaiety. War reminiscences which steered away from dangerous topics kept the talk going well enough, but Quincy began to wonder what was coming next. He felt certain that he had not been invited here purely for social purposes.

They had moved into the living room for coffee when Elinor asked abruptly, "Have you decided to return to New York, Jack? I hear you were taking another look at the canyon today, so I suppose you're now convinced that you don't have a chance."

"They didn't send me out here to make that kind of decision," he told her.

"What do you mean?"

"I'm on Midland's payroll as a construction engineer. They sent me out here to lay track, promising me materials and a crew. So far I haven't seen any trace of a crew and I've got a strong hunch that while your outfit controls the track between here and Pike Junction I'll get no materials. Nor do I have a right-of-way on which to lay track if I did get the men and materials. The company hasn't provided that any more than they have provided the other things."

"But you——"

"I don't have any responsibility in the matter. I'm here, ready to go to work. Until they make it possible for me to get busy I don't have to do a thing but wait. If I got itchy and went back to New York I'd be out of a job. This way I'm everything possible and I'm still on the payroll."

"You talk like a lawyer," Kell snapped.

"Everybody does—out here. Some of it is rubbing off on me."

Elinor broke in quickly as though scenting the ill-humor behind the remarks. "When you think about it we really do have a lot of legal angles in this situation. Your side is trying to void a lease. We're building track because a court decided that we have a right to use a certain piece of land—if we can reach it first. Not long ago your company earned the ill-feeling of the town by interpreting the law to suit itself. It's really quite complicated."

"You missed a couple of important ones," Quincy told her with a wry smile. "Such as delaying a court decision in order to gain time for some building. That fits."

"Anything wrong about that?" Kell snapped.

"I suppose not. But your company is a common carrier, obligated by law to carry all proper goods offered for shipment. You're holding up a lot of Midland material at Pike Junction instead of hauling it up here as you are supposed to do. Is that legal?"

Kell shrugged. "Prove that it isn't. The law says we must deliver but it doesn't say how soon. We'll haul the stuff up when we get good and ready."

"So I understood—and I'm really not complaining. Your evasion of the law will keep me in prosperous idleness."

His tone of smug satisfaction seemed to annoy Kell. "Maybe I could change that! Suppose we bring up a carload or two of rail? Then you'd have to fish or cut bait!"

"Very unfriendly thought," Quincy murmured, staring at the ceiling.

"Did you expect anything else?" the question was belligerent.

Quincy did not answer directly. He threw one long leg over the arm of his chair, aiming a small grin at Elinor. "Funny thing about Jeff and me," he drawled. "We never seemed to hit it off real nice."

"Good reason why not!" Kell growled.

Quincy had been studying him during the exchange, convinced that Kell was working up to a show of temper. Maybe he would say too much if he let his anger run away with him.

"Plenty of reason," he agreed with calm deliberation. "We tried to knock each other's blocks off when we hadn't been at the Academy a month. Jeff was sassy but I was bigger. All along it seemed to go that way, even when we stopped slugging and started battling each other for the smiles of a cute little gal named Elinor. Jeff never seemed to come out on top. I suppose he's got plenty of reason to hate me and it wouldn't hardly be human nature not to rawhide me now that he's got a chance."

Kell was sputtering before the goading speech was complete. He half-rose from his chair but his wife intervened hastily, her only word being a sharp, "Jeff!"

There was a clash of glances between them and Kell sank back, cursing under his breath. Quincy was a little disappointed but he realized that he had seen something worth knowing. His hunch that Elinor was boss was now more than a mere guess.

There was an interval of silence before Elinor turned to look Quincy squarely in the eye. "You're being deliberately malicious, Jack," she accused.

He nodded. "Sure. I'm down now. Jeff's operating a going concern while I'm bogged down. He married the girl —and I didn't. I've got reason to be malicious."

Kell exploded again. "What the hell do you mean by that?" he shouted. "Are you trying to say that I'm running this show because I married Elinor?"

"You made the connection," Quincy told him calmly. "I didn't; but I'll buy it."

Kell's face was white with anger as he came up out of his chair. For a moment Quincy thought that he was going to have a fight on his hands but then Elinor stepped in, again uttering only the one word, "Jeff!"

Her husband glared at her for only a split second. Then he turned and almost ran out of the room, slamming the door and pounding hard down the flight of bare steps.

Elinor watched him until the door slammed, making no comment. Finally she turned to ask, "Did you goad him into that deliberately, Jack?"

"It didn't take much goading."

"But you did, didn't you?"

"Yes. I had a feeling that his trouble was realization of his own unimportance. I think that's why he tried to run me out of town. He didn't want me to know that you were the real boss of this job."

"Then you believe I am?"

"Of course. Jeff is no better than he used to be when his non-coms had to repair his blunders for him. Now it's you who makes the decisions that he is incapable of making. You're the one who got him the job and you're the one who keeps him on it."

"How dare you tell me that?"

"Because it's true. You and I know each other too well to think that either of us can fool the other. Don't try."

She let herself sink wearily into her chair. "I ought to hate you for such talk," she murmured. "But I don't. Somehow I knew that it would turn out this way."

He didn't know what to say about that. The whole situation had become embarrassing. He had wanted to bait Jeff Kell because he hoped to get an unguarded statement from him. Instead he was in the position of being nasty to a woman who clearly held rather strong feelings toward him.

"I think I'd better get out of here," he said awkwardly. "I'm sorry I came. Sorry I said what I did."

She met his glance squarely once more. "It's all right, Jack. We've been honest with each other all along, no matter how mistaken I was in the past. It's all right to keep it that way."

"Thanks."

"Then tell me honestly—if it had been you instead of Jeff that I married would you resent my interference with the job?"

Quincy smiled thinly. "You know it wouldn't happen. If I had the job I wouldn't need you to run it for me."

She gave him just a faint ghost of a smile. "Can't catch you in any trap, can I? But then I didn't expect to. I couldn't even trap you into marrying me."

"A man makes mistakes sometimes."

"You think that was one of yours?"

"I thought so as soon as we parted."

"And you still think so?"

"Whoa! You're married to Jeff Kell. At this point I stop talking."

"Maybe you don't need to say any more." Her voice had dropped almost to a whisper as she uttered the words.

Quincy moved toward the door, reaching for the hat he had left on a table. "I've already said too much, I'm afraid. And I've undoubtedly stayed too long. Jeff wasn't very smart to go out and leave me alone with you."

She took a step toward him but he didn't wait to see what she intended to do. Life was already too complicated and he didn't propose to let this particular tangle get any worse. He almost fled down the stairs.

He knew that he ought to find a way to make some kind of contact with O'Hara in order to learn what Muldoon and Margaret O'Hara had accomplished. With time a vital factor he had to keep his new allies moving. Still he hesitated as he stood in the darkness outside the railroad building, trying to settle his own thoughts. He had not learned what he had wanted to learn but he had certainly picked up some sharp ideas about Jeff and Elinor. The whole trouble was that they were ideas which might detract from his own ability to concentrate.

After a few minutes he turned and walked slowly along the darkened railroad tracks, forcing himself to consider the whole situation as impersonally as possible. It took some little time but after a half hour of pacing the rail yards he knew what he had to do. He had to stay completely away from Elinor Kell. Otherwise he might never make good his newly planned strategy.

It wasn't much of a conclusion but it made him feel a little better, so he moved back toward the main street, intending to stop at the hotel and then go on to make a cautious approach to the O'Hara establishment.

Because he was preoccupied he was not as alert as he should have been. There was only a second or two for him to realize that three dark figures were hurling themselves at him from the mouth of a narrow alley. He turned to meet the attack but could not ward off so much unexpected fury. Something pounded down hard against his skull and he felt his senses reeling. A second blow fell and so did he, out cold.

Chapter 7

CONSCIOUSNESS came back slowly and reluctantly. For some minutes all he knew was that he was uncomfortable. Then the discomfort could be identified as an aching head. Still later he reached the conclusion that he was in bed in a darkened room. Somehow it didn't seem worth the trouble to figure out what room.

After a while objects began to take shape in the gloom and he knew that some of the ache was easing. The dizziness which had troubled his vision was not so bad now. He saw that the shades had been drawn to keep out what looked like bright sunlight, and then he knew that he was in his own hotel room. He put a shaky hand to his aching head and felt the neat bandage that was there. That brought back the memories of the attack.

They were confused memories but finally he got them sorted out. Somebody had been waiting for him in that dark alley—last night, he supposed it must have been. Three men had caught him by surprise and hammered him to the ground. It gave him several questions to think about. Who had slugged him? Why? How had he got back into the hotel? Who had put the bandage on his head?

Part of the answer came promptly. The door opened and a head appeared, evidently someone making a cautious inspection of the patient before entering the room. He assumed that it must be a friend so he announced, "I'm awake. Come on in." He tried to make himself sound cheerful but was much annoyed to hear the tremor in his own voice.

The door opened all the way and Elinor Kell stepped in. Behind her a little man with a straggling mustache pushed forward, a black bag and a bustling manner marking him as a physician.

"Quiet," the little man ordered as he came through the doorway. "No talking and don't try to sit up!"

51

Quincy watched him in the lightened gloom. "Bad as that?" he murmured.

"Your skull must be thick," the doctor grumbled. "Lucky it's not a fracture. Now keep quiet while I look you over."

Elinor put the shade up enough so that the doctor had light for his examination. Quincy remained motionless while the work went on, his mind clear enough now to read worry in the dark eyes of the woman. He wanted to think that she was worrying about his condition but he had a feeling that her real worry was over the possibility that Jeff had been responsible for the assault.

Finally the doctor seemed satisfied. He had grunted and clicked his tongue all through the examination but his last grunt was a pleased one. "Not too bad," he announced. "Got a bad gash on top of the head and a lump that could be troublesome. Concussion maybe but no fracture. You'll need plenty of rest. Stay in bed for three or four days. Lucky you got a hard head."

He went to the door and spoke briskly. "Come in, Sheriff. You may ask the patient the necessary questions. Three minutes is your limit."

The bulky form of Sheriff Naylor ambled into the room and again Quincy had the feeling that he was looking at a person who was distinctly uneasy. Again he had a hunch to go with the first impression. He thought that Naylor had to ask questions because it was his legal duty, but that the fat man didn't really want to learn any answers.

"What happened to you?" Naylor asked abruptly.

"Three men rushed me at the mouth of an alley near the hotel. I suppose they hit me over the head."

"Recognize any of them?"

"No." He was sure that the answer made the lawman feel easier.

"Got any idea why they jumped you?"

"Maybe. Could be it was part of the deal I reported before. I'm not sure."

"Anything more to tell me?"

"No."

Sheriff Naylor didn't even glance at the other two occupants of the room. He simply turned and went out. Quincy watched the departing bulk before asking a question of his own.

"How did I get here?"

"A workman saw you in the alley this morning." It was Elinor who did the answering. "You must have been bleeding there most of the night. They brought you to your room as soon as they knew who you were. The hotel man sent a message to Jeff and me, knowing that you had been to dinner with us last night. He didn't know of anyone else in town who might be friendly to you. Jeff had gone out on the job but I came over at once."

"Been here all day," the doctor grunted. "Good nurse."

"Doctor Summerall was afraid the exposure might bring on pneumonia. You lost a lot of blood and would be very weak."

"Thanks to both of you," Quincy said soberly. "Looks like I fell into good hands."

"Don't talk any more," Summerall ordered. "You're not out of the woods yet. Give him the medicine I showed you, Mrs. Kell, and keep him quiet until I see him again."

He went out almost as abruptly as Sheriff Naylor had done.

Quincy asked one more question as Elinor came toward him with a vial and a spoon. "You're staying here?"

"Of course. You need me."

He didn't think it smart to press the point. It still seemed more than likely that she suspected her husband of organizing the attack and she was doing what she could to compensate. Maybe her motives were more personal but Quincy decided not to discuss it. For the moment he was more concerned with the awkward and rather ridiculous position in which he found himself. His one chance of success in the canyon struggle was to make a quick and unexpected move. Today he ought to be organizing that move, even getting it under way. Instead he was helpless, completely cut off from his new lieutenants and actually under the observation and care of the enemy. It was enough to make his head ache worse.

Elinor refused to talk after giving him the medicine and presently he dozed off, awakening some time later to ask another question. "What time is it?"

She looked up with a smile. "You sound better—and it's about three o'clock."

"Afternoon?"

"Yes."

"How long was I unconscious before I woke up and talked with you and the doctor?"

"We don't know when you were attacked. It was just after noon when Doctor Summerall was here."

"I must have been out for a bit over twelve hours," he calculated. "Quite a wallop I took."

"Several wallops," she amended soberly. "If you haven't realized it yet you are bruised in a number of places. The doctor thinks you were kicked after you were knocked out." Her voice was not quite steady and again Quincy had a feeling that she was considering the attack in terms of a specific attacker.

"Could you estimate what time it occurred?" she asked, changing the subject quickly.

"About eleven, I guess. It was nearly ten when I left your place. I did some walking and some thinking before I headed back here."

He dozed again, fitfully and with his head still aching. Once when he awakened he found a man at the door talking to Elinor and he caught the sound of a vaguely familiar voice. He was about to drift off to sleep once more when he realized who the visitor was.

"If that's Mr. Pettigrew," he called, "I'd like to talk to him for a minute or two."

Elinor turned questioningly. "You feel strong enough?"

"Sure. That last nap helped. Anyway I ought to talk to the only man in town who dares to have any dealings with me. He can handle a couple of chores for me while I'm flat on my back here."

"Of course," Elinor said hastily. "I forgot that Mr. Pettigrew was your banker. I think I'll seize this opportunity to run over home for a few minutes. Please don't let him become excited, Mr. Pettigrew."

The banker waited until she had closed the door behind her. Then he came across to the bedside and asked abruptly, "Are you able to talk and think clearly?"

"Pretty good, I guess. Why?"

"Because I've been hearing a crazy story today from people who want me to advance them money on your account. It seemed mighty fishy to have a thing like that come along when you were reported out of your head. I refused."

"Properly so, I'm sure. But if the applicant was a man

named Muldoon or one of the O'Haras you'll have to change your decision."

Pettigrew looked surprised. "O'Hara and Muldoon were the two," he agreed.

"I'd better tell you. This is very much a secret, particularly since I must depend on them to make their own arrangements without me for a few days. I think we have a plan that might work. I've reported on it by mail to Elias Bostwick but in the interval before we can get a reply from him I'm assuming responsibility. Give O'Hara or Muldoon —or Miss Margaret O'Hara—any financial assistance they request. I'll put that order in writing if you insist but for the present I'd much prefer to avoid the risk of doing anything in writing."

"What about a credit letter or check which I could deposit to the account of Mr. O'Hara? Banks have rules, you know."

"Very well," Quincy said wearily. "Make it out and I'll sign it. How much did they ask for?"

"A thousand dollars drawing account."

"Make it five. If they do a decent job they'll need more than that."

Pettigrew went to the bureau and used it as a desk to draw up the paper. Quincy signed it with a rather shaky hand but the banker didn't question it.

It was clear that the thin man didn't propose to risk his professional dignity by asking questions so Quincy took the initiative. "I'm depending on you, Mr. Pettigrew," he said seriously. "It's very important that O'Hara get every chance to help me, particularly since I'm unable to act for myself. It's equally important that no one know what he is doing."

The banker showed signs of interest. "Then you have some kind of plan?"

"We do. Yesterday I thought I had a very good chance. Now I don't know. Everything depends on people I scarcely know. They won't dare to make contact with me so it would be an immense help if you would stand ready to pass along any messages they may wish to give me. Naturally we'll protect your position just as I'm asking you to protect theirs."

Pettigrew chuckled dryly. "Sounds like you've got the hang of things around here. I'll play along. Maybe we can help to break this dirty crew that's running Machete."

"Fine. The first step is to do anything you can to arrange for O'Hara to sell some scrap material to a man named Muldoon. Midland will finance any part of the deal. Get the details from O'Hara; I'm feeling pretty groggy again."

He lay back and closed his eyes against the pain. He didn't even know when Pettigrew left the room. When he awoke again he was alone and it was dark. He found that thinking came a little easier so he tried to work out plans as best he could without knowing what was going on outside. After a while he even tried to sit up but the effort was painful and he went back to sleep again.

It was daylight again when he awoke from the nap feeling really refreshed. He was just in time to see Elinor come in. She gave him a cheery-enough greeting but her manner was restrained and he suspected that she had been having some words with Jeff. That was to be expected, he realized. Jeff would not like the idea of having her act as nurse for Jack Quincy.

"You shouldn't do this," he told her seriously. "I'll be all right now. You'll make me feel mighty awkward getting indebted to the enemy like this."

She came over to take his pulse, using a remarkably long time in getting the chore accomplished. Finally she smiled and said, "Pretty normal—and don't ever call me the enemy again. You know better than that."

He preferred not to reply, taking refuge in his own miseries and pretending to ignore her. Actually it wasn't too hard to pretend weakness. His head felt better but the body aches were beginning to make themselves known every time he ventured to move. Those thugs in the alley had really kicked him around after knocking him senseless. He just hoped that some day he would find out who was responsible.

He put in a pretty uncomfortable day. His ribs and his head hurt most of the time. He was uneasily aware of the passage of valuable time. Pacific crews would be closing in on Rock Corner, ready to push on up the canyon to the Keyhole. Instead of rushing the job of trying to forestall them he was flat on his back in a hotel room.

Elinor's open solicitude didn't help his state of mind. She was making it very clear that she was concerned about him, fixing his pillow every few minutes and fussing over him until he took pains to pretend sleep every time she came near his bed. Perhaps sympathy for him was back of her concern—or it might be remorse because she believed her husband was responsible—but Quincy had a strong hunch that there was more to it than that. Memories were too clear in his own thoughts for him to think that Elinor could ignore or forget the past. He simply couldn't afford to let the old emotions return. Not when Elinor was married to another man—even Jeff Kell.

Banker Pettigrew came into the room that evening almost as soon as Elinor left it. He had slicked the gray hair over his bald spot a little more carefully than usual and something in his air of business hinted at brisk cheerfulness.

"I waited until the lady cleared out," he greeted in a conspiratorial whisper. "Lucky I did. It let me hear a few words between her and her husband. He met her in the lobby when she went out."

"Is he sore because she's staying with me?" Quincy asked.

"Likely enough." Pettigrew chuckled gleefully. He seemed to be enjoying himself to a degree Quincy had not suspected would be possible for him. "What he was real sharp about was findin' out who'd been in to see ye."

"Why?"

"Seems like a man named Muldoon put a crew to work this mornin' at tearin' up the old coal-mine tracks. Kell seemed to think it might be some of your doin'."

"Then Muldoon started the job?"

"Sure. I imagine the O'Hara girl prodded him into it. She's a go-getter, that girl."

"You've been keeping an eye on things?" Quincy pushed up on an elbow long enough to get an assortment of pains and then lay down again.

"I play it shady," Pettigrew told him with a broad wink. "I dropped in at O'Hara's this morning to make a small purchase and managed to pass your message along. That seemed to be quite enough. Miss O'Hara came to the bank this afternoon—when several other people were there—and left a deposit for me to record. Later I found her note among the papers. O'Hara has sold the old coal line to a certain Elk Ridge Mining Company and has a paper authorizing it to be turned over to a certain Martin Muldoon who will remove the materials for transportation to the company's property."

Quincy grinned. "Sounds like my volunteer army is operating quite well while the commander loafs."

"Better than well," Pettigrew informed him. "At supper time tonight I heard the gossip going around. A work crew started today at the point where the old track crosses the northeast trail. They've worked in both directions from the crossing, piling up ties and rails in convenient centers but not attempting to load anything. Muldoon has apparently talked freely but vaguely. According to him the material is to be hauled some distance to the north and they don't propose to move any of it until a complete wagon train can be assembled. He is likewise vague about the location of this Elk Ridge Mining Company. He's just the hauling contractor, he claims, and he doesn't know anything about the company itself."

"Excellent. I feel better already. But you say Kell was suspicious?"

"I think so. He seemed to relax a little when your nurse told him that no one but Doctor Summerall had been in to see you. She was almost annoyed that he should think you had anything to do with removing those rails."

"She didn't mention that you were here last night?"

"No. I think she'd forgotten it. That was why I kept out of sight and didn't come up here until they left. No use letting them suspect anything."

Quincy grinned again. "You're not the old fogey you try to make out, Pettigrew. You're having a lot of fun out of this, aren't you?"

The banker chuckled self-consciously. "I suppose I am. It's kinda fun to stick a pin in the folks that have been having things their own way for so long."

"Well keep sticking. You're a key man in this deal—and it begins to look like I picked a smart one for key man."

Elinor did not arrive until nearly nine o'clock on the following morning and when she came in Kell was with her. Evidently their tempers had been toned down for the occasion because Jeff was very genial although a trifle smug.

"I just came in to annoy you a little, Jack," he announced with a show of geniality. "The westbound freight this morning will bring in a carload of rails and two of ties for you."

"Thanks," Quincy told him dryly. "I'll have them brought up here to my room. Company for the lonely nights."

"You don't sound appreciative, Jack."

"Stop it! I'm in no mood for that kind of jokes. Is this a formal announcement of the arrival of freight?"

"Call it that if you want to be stuffy."

"I just want to be legal. I refuse to accept the shipment. That's also formal. Now you can't charge me any demurrage."

Kell laughed. "Smart, aren't you? I don't care a hoot about demurrage. All I'm trying to do is make sure that I can prove our attempt to deliver. Now we have no further responsibility for the materials in the Pike Junction yards."

"That's your game, eh?" Quincy growled. "I can change that with a wire."

"Not over our wires, mister."

"Stop it, Jeff!" Elinor cut in. "The doctor said that Jack was to have quiet. He's not getting it when you stand there and bait him. Get on out to the gorge and see about repairing that landslide."

"And take the rails with you!" Quincy added. "You might as well have them. The only rails I'll have dealing with for some time to come will be bed rails!"

Kell seemed to think that was a fine joke. At least he was laughing loudly when he went out. Quincy didn't even dare risk a glance at Elinor. He was afraid she might see through his elaborate pose of pessimism. For the moment it seemed like a fine idea to let Jeff crow—and to let him think that John Quincy was not interested in railroad materials, either new or used. If that remark about a landslide in the gorge meant anything it definitely hinted that Midland's new crew had a little more time in which to prepare their coup. An unguarded grin at this moment might ruin the whole show.

Chapter 8

THAT AFTERNOON Doctor Summerall came in to examine the patient and gave a cheerful verdict. The real danger was past. Only bruises remained and they would respond to more rest. The scalp wound was already healing and the other head injury did not seem to be at all serious.

"Three days and you'll do," he pronounced.

"Three more days in bed and I'll go loco," Quincy retorted.

"Then get up tomorrow. But don't try to do anything more than walk around the room. You'll find out for yourself that you'll have some mighty weak knees."

There was a rather strained silence after the physician left. It was Quincy who broke it. "You'd better not come in any more, Elinor. I appreciate your kindness, of course, but it'll be better if I go it alone now."

"Afraid to trust the enemy?" she inquired with a smile that didn't quite hide her real thoughts.

"You know it isn't that. You still look like the girl I once loved. That makes it all the harder to remember that you are another man's wife. Even discounting the prospect of local gossip it adds up to a bad risk."

She made no attempt to evade the issue. "I suppose you're right, Jack. It's as hard for me as it is for you. Harder, perhaps, because I have to treat you as an enemy."

"Meaning that I don't have to do the same thing?"

"It's not quite the same. I must be an active enemy of yours because I'm in a position to hurt you. In your case your helplessness keeps you from having that particular pang."

"Maybe I wouldn't be so sentimental."

"No matter. Let's just remember that you flattered my feminine ego by reminding me that I still have an attraction for you. A woman always likes to be flattered, you know."

He laughed with her, willing to adopt the lighter note.

60

"More flattery you certainly do not need. Anyway I'll be on safer ground to remind you that I'm the enemy."

"No need to be," she said, her mood dropping away. "Other railroads need good construction engineers. You needn't remain with a company that puts you in an impossible position. I'm sure Pacific could use you."

Again there was a frank meeting of glances. He preferred to ignore what he saw, passing it off with a vague, "Thanks for the suggestion. I'll keep it in mind."

She didn't turn away for a full minute. Then there was a smile on her full lips as she moved across to pick up her cloak. "The patient is now discharged," she murmured solemnly. "One of these days I'll be sending in my bill for nursing services."

He had an answer for that but he decided that it would be smarter not to make it.

The interview left him feeling a little guilty. Elinor had been frank about the situation while he had been forced to use deceit. It bothered him most of the evening in spite of his efforts to convince himself that he had had no choice in the matter. Elinor and Pacific had all of the other advantages while his only hole card was the proposed move against the Keyhole. A hole card had to be kept secret at all costs.

It didn't help that Pettigrew made no report. Quincy knew that the banker was probably being discreet, remaining away in order to avoid arousing suspicion. If everything was going well there would be no reason for a report. Still he spent an uneasy evening, not dropping off to sleep until long after the town was quiet.

He was awakened shortly before noon when the hotel proprietor came in. The little man grinned amiably as Quincy sat up in bed, half-apologetic as he explained, "Your nurse didn't show up so I thought I'd better look in. Everything all right?"

"Seems so. I'm hungry, if that's a good sign."

"Want me to bring up a meal?"

"Good idea. I'll get out of bed and try my legs while you're doing it."

He took plenty of time with it, discovering that Doctor Summerall had been accurate in his forecast. It took a little time for his legs to feel like anything but old rubber, but he steadied a little as he moved around, even getting into some clothes before the tray of food came up. In the process of dressing he discovered that he had not been robbed, though his assailants had had plenty of time to do it. That was significant. If robbery was not the motive for such a vicious beating it meant that someone had a real personal grudge. There were only three people in Machete who could reasonably be expected to hold such a grudge. Kell, Winters and Ames. And there had been three assailants.

The meal helped a lot and late in the afternoon he decided that he would try his legs on the stairs. He made it to the lobby but didn't go out, content to rest a while and then go back to his room. There was no point in being hasty; for the moment he couldn't accomplish anything in town so it would be smarter to get his strength back before making any move.

Another night's sleep brought back a feeling of something like normality, and immediately after breakfast he went out into another of those crisp April days like the one which had marked his arrival in Machete. He hoped that this day would not be as baffling as that first one but he knew that he could expect no relaxation. The race against time was already in progress, even though its start was still a secret.

When he left the hotel he noticed the man who came out of the barber shop across the street. A hundred yards down the street he stopped to lean against a hitch rack, fully aware that his legs were far from normal, and noticed the man again. This time the fellow was showing great interest in a dusty store window. Quincy studied him with care, alert to the chance that Pacific might be suspicious enough to have put a watcher on his movements. He did not recall having seen the man before but could not be sure. Maybe that was why this particular individual had been selected for the job. He was of medium height, medium weight and nondescript coloring, the sort of man who would pass unnoticed almost anywhere.

It was fairly easy to check the hunch and within ten minutes Quincy knew that he was under surveillance. That was going to make matters a bit more difficult. He couldn't risk any contact with the O'Hara's.

Sight of the jail and sheriff's office gave him an idea, so

he turned in at the little frame structure, finding Sheriff Naylor in the same semi-recumbent position as on the other visit.

The fat man looked annoyed but managed to offer a gruff salute. "Up and about, hey? Sorry but I ain't got a thing to tell you."

"Not even a guess?"

Naylor snorted. "It ain't my business to make guesses."

Quincy shrugged and pointed to his own bandaged head. "I suppose not. But I didn't come in for that reason. My hat's missing. Did it get picked up?"

The fat man's relief was still mixed with suspicion but he nodded. "I got it. Kept it for evidence but I don't reckon it's goin' to do us no good. You still had it on your head when they picked you up. It was plumb full of blood but mebbe it saved gittin' a busted skull."

He went to a closet and brought out the hat, displaying its crushed and bloody crown. "Total loss, I'd call it."

Quincy nodded. "Might as well throw it away. I wasn't robbed, so I've got money enough to buy a new one."

He wanted to see whether the lawman would comment on the significant point he had mentioned, but Naylor surprised him. There was a flash of interest in the man's eyes, hidden swiftly as he growled, "Lots of hat places in town. You might try O'Hara. He's the best general outfitter we got."

Quincy knew that he was being watched for a reaction so he made his own reply as casual as possible. It was disturbing to realize that someone had scented the connection between himself and O'Hara, so he knew that he would have to be doubly careful. "Most people in Machete don't seem keen on doing any kind of business with me. I guess I'll just wear my bandage for a few days. It'll be hat enough."

"Aw, folks ain't that skittish," Naylor told him. "I ain't doin' nothin' right now so I'll go along with you. O'Hara won't kick up if I'm with you. You know where his place is at, don't you?"

Quincy tried to look thoughtful. "The name sounds vaguely familiar. I think I hired a horse from somebody of that name when I first rode up into the canyon. A relation?"

"Same Irishman. He's got a livery and a store. Sells everything from petticoats to plows. Daughter mostly runs the stable for him."

He was coming around the desk as he spoke, moving with an eagerness that seemed completely foreign. Quincy knew what it meant. Naylor had a definite idea that there was a connection between O'Hara and the Midland engineer. He had failed to get a reaction from his opening remark but now he had a better idea. He proposed to force the play, going along with Quincy to the store in order to watch a meeting.

"Nice of you," Quincy told him smoothly. There was nothing to do but to play along. Refusal would only add to the suspicion. He had to gamble that O'Hara would rise to the occasion.

The nondescript trailer was on the street when they went out and Quincy was interested to see the signal passed by the sheriff. It was just another indication that Machete's law was more than merely careless. Sheriff Naylor knew exactly what was going on.

Quincy wanted to make a comment but he refrained, remembering that one of his few advantages was in knowing more than the enemy thought he knew. A word now would cause a change in spies. It was much easier to know who was tailing him.

He rested four times on the way to O'Hara's place, partly because he needed the rests and partly because he wanted to make a point of his own weakness. Still he was apprehensive when they entered the store, all too aware that the sheriff would be looking for even the smallest slip.

The place was empty but the clanging of the door bell brought a quick sound of movement from the rear. It was Margaret O'Hara who came through from the living quarters, her quick smile changing to a little frown as she stared at Quincy. For a moment he was afraid she had spilled the beans, but then she spoke and he realized that she knew exactly what she was doing.

"You're the man who was hurt the other night, aren't you?" she asked. "And you're the same one who was here to get a horse! I remember now."

Quincy decided that she was a good actress as well as a good businesswoman. If he hadn't known different he would have sworn that she was both surprised and pleased at the identification. Playing it very smart, he thought. Everyone in town must know of the attack upon him. It would not have been reasonable to pretend total ignorance.

"Same man," he acknowledged. "Now I'm the man who came here to get a hat. My other one was on my head when this happened." He pointed to the bandage.

"How terrible! What kind of hat did you want?"

"Just a hat. Something for ordinary wear. Size seven and a quarter. I hope your sizes are accurate; I can't try it on while I'm wearing all this muslin on my noggin."

She laughed politely and assured him that he could depend on the size markings being correct. He glanced at Sheriff Naylor as the girl turned away toward a rack. The fat man looked disappointed but he was still watching.

Miss O'Hara seemed completely preoccupied with the hat when she brought it back. It was a flat-crowned black felt more reminiscent of a cattleman than an engineer. "Something like this?" she asked.

"A little out of my line," Quincy commented, "but maybe it's a good idea to have that chin strap. While it has to perch on top of a bandage it'll probably need an anchor."

"It will if you're going to be riding."

"He'll be ridin' trains if he's smart," Naylor growled. "This town just ain't healthy for him."

"I'm not that smart," Quincy retorted. "But I might be smart enough to start protecting my health with a gun. Does this establishment sell firearms?"

"We sell just about everything," the girl told him, "but maybe we can offer you a deal." She winked at Sheriff Naylor and confided, "I heard that this gent didn't come back to us the second time he wanted to hire a horse. Bud Mayhew got the business. We can't have that kind of thing happening so I'll rent him a gun along with a horse next time."

"Who's thinking there's going to be a next time?" Naylor demanded.

"In business you always look for a next time. Today takes care of itself; tomorrow's profit is the one to worry about."

"You're doin' all right," Naylor told her. "Your old man made a good thing out of peddlin' that old coal-mine track."

"Not so good," she denied. "He got a tip on that new mine to the north and was all set to sell them the lot.

Then Marty Muldoon turned out to be the fly in the ointment. He'd gotten his hooks into the deal and corralled every team in the county. Father had the rail, good for nothing but scrap unless he could find a buyer. Muldoon had the transportation tied up. They finally made a dicker so that both of them will make a fair profit, but there was some hard Irish language exchanged before they shook hands on it." She seemed vastly amused by the memory.

Quincy had turned away, pretending to examine the hat in a better light. Naylor obligingly asked the question that was in Quincy's mind. "How soon are they hauling the stuff? Last I heard they was just pilin' it up along the northeast pass trail."

"I wouldn't be knowing," she replied, dropping into the thick brogue. "The O'Hara won't let it go whilst his money ain't been paid and you may lay to that!"

"But I hear Muldoon's got his wagons ready to load."

She shrugged. "Ask the pair of them. Likely they're both trying to find some dirty way to cheat each other."

"Just my luck to get knocked on the head at the wrong time," Quincy grumbled, returning with the hat. "I'd have bought the rail myself if I'd known it was on the market."

"You're not figgerin' to buck the tiger, are you?" Naylor asked.

"I would if I could. I came out here to lay rail. Our company needs a line from several miles east of town on through here to the west. It would have helped if I could put some down anywhere in that stretch."

"Be a waste of rail, wouldn't it?" Miss O'Hara inquired idly.

"Maybe. But I'd be doing my job. I'm not supposed to lay track in any particular place and it's none of my business if they gave me stupid instructions—but why talk about it? I don't have the rail."

They completed the hat-buying and went out, Naylor leaving as soon as they reached the street. Quincy was interested to note that the medium man had taken over the tailing once more so he wandered on back to the hotel, willing enough to sit down and rest. It had been quite an afternoon he had planned for himself but he knew that his plans would have to be altered. After the strenuous morning he didn't have the energy to do anything more.

It annoyed him to feel the weakness but he consoled himself with the thought that he had fooled Naylor. Or perhaps it would be better to say that Margaret O'Hara had fooled him. In any event things were shaping up. The rails and ties were ready for transport. The next step would be to find a way to order the movement without giving the show away.

He slept most of the afternoon but felt well enough to go down to the hotel dining room for supper. His bandaged head was attracting attention, he knew, but it was not the hostile attention he had seen on all sides when he first appeared in town. On the street during the morning he had felt something of the same impression but now he was sure. People were less hostile now. They were not risking any show of friendliness but the air of resentment was gone. He didn't know whether is was merely sympathy or a more serious reaction against the highhanded methods of the men who had been running the town.

Pettigrew came in, greeting him loudly and with a show of wry humor. "Up and about, eh?" the little man exclaimed. "That's good. Thought for a spell I might be going to lose my best depositor. How do you feel?"

Quincy motioned him to a seat. "Have supper with me," he invited. "It gets tiresome eating alone all the time. Maybe folks won't hold it against you now that I'm too helpless to be a corrupting influence."

They kept up a pretense of idle banter but at the first opportunity Pettigrew murmured, "They got a good mile of track up now. Twenty wagons ready to move in for the ties and about ten flat beds that can handle rails. Muldoon figures to use mules to carry most of the rail, one or two rails to each animal. When should they start to load?"

"Twenty wagons!" Quincy whispered. "That's plenty more than I thought he'd get. Tell them to load tomorrow. Make it look like they're planning to pull out in a wagon train the following morning."

"You be able to take over by then?"

"I'm sure going to try, but even if I can't it sounds like the job is in good hands. I'll be around to see you in the morning."

Chapter 9

QUINCY TOOK plenty of time about getting out on the street next morning. With a full day ahead of him he knew that he had to avoid the appearance of haste so he deliberately dawdled over breakfast in the hotel and lounged along the street as though satisfied to enjoy the sunshine. Because he was deliberate with his loafing he had plenty of chance to see things. The inconspicuous man who had shadowed him on the previous day was still back there. Today the tailer was getting a certain amount of joshing as he moved along. Somehow the town's attitude had altered.

The first stop was at the little white frame house which served Doctor Summerall as home and office. The physician was there and he made a quick check of his patient, pronouncing a satisfactory verdict.

"Just don't pick any more fights," he warned. "Even a real thick skull can't take too much."

Quincy laughed, paid him, and went out. His shadow was standing in front of a shop some fifty feet away but there was another man at the gate of Summerall's little house-yard, a gangling, stoop-shouldered man whose full beard and shaggy brows made him look like an unkempt animal of some sort. He was a bit ragged about the knees and elbows but his clothing was clean and there was an air of dogged determination about him which marked him as something more than the hobo he appeared.

"You-all Mister Quincy?" he inquired without ceremony, his drawl so exaggerated that for a moment Quincy thought it might be assumed.

"I am. Who wants me?"

"I'm Jason Applegate, sir. About a fortnight ago I headed out this way because I got me a job with a railroad. Man in St. Louis handed me a ticket and told me to come out here and report to a gent name of Quincy. Last night another man at a place called Pike Junction told us it was too late to get to you. Four-five other boys took him at his word and headed back east again. I kinda had a feelin' he wasn't on the level so I come on out. Didn't cost nothin' more bein' as I already had the ticket."

Quincy studied him as he spoke, wondering if this could be a Pacific trick. Maybe they wanted to put one of their agents in a spot where he could do some real spying.

"Who hired you?" he asked briefly.

"Fellow name of Olmstead."

"Describe him."

The lanky man looked up, clear gray eyes narrowed a little as he drawled, "Funny question, mister. If you don't trust me that's your business. I'll just hunt me another job."

"I'll lay it out for you," Quincy told him quietly. "See that man back there on the corner? He's watching me every step I make. We've got the makings of a small war in these parts and the enemy has already put both thugs and spies to work on me. You could be their next move—and I can't afford to be easy. I guess you understand that."

The lanky man grinned. "Sounds like old times. That Yankee talk of yours says you wasn't on the same side as me but I reckon we got some of the same ideas. So this here Olmstead was a tall man with bushy sideburns. Bald on top but brushy around the sides. Big mole on his left cheek and talked Yank like yourself. Went strong for fancy weskits."

"How much advance pay did he give you?"

"Just a ticket. Claimed you was paymaster out here."

"And you still want to work for me even when you know that you may get yourself tangled up in a fight?"

Applegate laughed. "Shucks, mister. I never had much of a trade only fightin'. That don't scare me a little bit."

"Right. You're on. Regular rate is five dollars a day."

The lanky man grinned a little more widely. "Suits me fine. Olmstead only offered three."

"Five," Quincy repeated. "More if you're worth it. When are you ready to start?"

"I ain't a-goin' nowhere but here. Got any orders?"

"Know mules?"

"I'm from Arkansas—if you ain't guessed it already. I fought the war with General Jo Shelby and when I wasn't shootin' Yanks I was runnin' off their mules."

Quincy grinned. "I've heard about Shelby's campaigns. I think you'll do. I want to buy a good freight wagon with a six-mule team. Suppose you do the buying for me. I'll go along to pay the bill. Right with you?"

Applegate looked surprised but nodded. "I reckon I kin dicker a mite," he said.

They moved off in the direction of Bud Mayhew's livery stable, Quincy explaining a part of the situation as they went along. He didn't go into details about plans but he let it be known that he was planning to get out of town and stay for a while. They were going to stock the new wagon with camp supplies, food and other materials. Applegate was to make any suggestions as they went on with their buying.

They were on reasonably good terms by the time they turned in at Bud Mayhew's stable, Applegate even turning to wave a genial hand at the man who had trailed them up the street. The Arkansan seemed to be quite elated at the sort of job he had picked, bracing himself visibly as he prepared to demonstrate his prowess as a bargainer.

It proved to be an entertaining process. Applegate argued and scoffed until he seemed on the verge of a real brawl with the short, stocky Mayhew. Eventually, however, they shook hands on a deal which looked like a good one to Quincy. At that point Quincy left them and walked back to the bank while Applegate took over the duties of getting the team harnessed and ready. He did not see his private shadow this time, so he assumed that the man had gone to report the new arrival in the enemy ranks.

In spite of Pettigrew's expressed fears he drew out five thousand dollars, mostly in ten-dollar bills, stuffing money in every pocket so as to distribute the bulk. Then he went back to the livery and paid the astonished Mayhew in cash, careful to get bills of sale for each item in the deal.

When they drove away, Applegate handling the team with something of a flourish, Quincy knew that several men were watching. Evidently the word had been passed that the Midland engineer was on the move and was to be observed with due care.

At the next stop, a harness shop, he bought saddles and other gear for two horses, doing his own buying this time while Applegate stayed with the wagon. A hardware store further reduced his cash capital when he purchased two shotguns, a Winchester rifle, and a good stock of ammunition for each type of weapon. He would have preferred to give O'Hara the business but he couldn't afford to concentrate too much on that establishment. He had to make O'Hara's just one of a series of stops.

Between the hardware store and O'Hara's he spotted two familiar figures on horseback. Ames and Winters were letting their horses idle in the street, not even pretending to be doing anything except watching the preparations Quincy was making. Both men were armed and it was obvious that they were issuing orders to the other watchers. Quincy called his new employee's attention to the situation. "Might be they're planning to hijack us after we get out of town. The pair on horseback go for that sort of thing. Be a good idea if you'd break out some firearms while I'm making my next stop."

The defense preparations were serious enough but at the same time it kept Applegate busy for the O'Hara visit. In case the man was not as loyal as Quincy had decided to believe he was there would be a point in keeping him ignorant of the O'Hara connection.

They turned into the lane, pulling up in the open space in front of the livery stable. Margaret came into view at once, dressed much as she had been on the occasion of their first meeting. She brushed a wisp of shiny hair out of her eyes with a forearm, squinting up at Quincy as though seeing him for the first time.

"Somethin' I could be doin' for you?" she inquired.

"Got a couple of good saddle horses for sale?"

"We got them. Better light down and take a look."

She led the way to the corral, ignoring the rider who had come back into the lane and halted. At this stage of the game Pacific seemed content to let Quincy know that he was being watched. Margaret commented on the fact when they were out of earshot of Applegate. "Could be they're trying to get your nerve," she murmured. "Or maybe they don't care whether you know what they're up to."

She pointed into the corral as she spoke and he went close to the bars, peering in with studious care as he replied, "If we can make the move fast it won't matter. How much of that track is ready for shipment?"

"A mile or so. We could move twenty wagons on short notice."

"Found anybody to handle the block-and-tackle rigs?"

"One man knows something about it. He also claims he knows you. His name is something like Schnitzel-heimer but around here they call him Dutch Fritz. Father says he was in your regiment during the war."

Quincy nodded, pointing through into the corral as though inquiring about the specific pony. "I remember him. Good man—but we'll need more. Anything I ought to buy from you in addition to a couple of saddle ponies?"

"You can always haul along some extra rations. We've smuggled out everything else we thought you'd need. Muldoon has quite a supply dump on the ridge."

"Good. Pick out two good broncs and charge me plenty for them. Then get my new assistant to carry out any supplies you want to sell us. I think he's all right but don't tip the hand."

"You want that gun I promised you when we were playing games with the sheriff?"

"No. I don't want to risk starting any violence. This game seems to be one of seeing how close we can skate to the edge of legality without going over the side. I don't want to make the first slip."

"What about the other side? That attack on you wasn't your idea of staying legal, was it?"

"But I can't prove Pacific was responsible."

"I suppose not, but town gossip says Kell ordered it and helped to carry it out."

"With a little help from Ames and Winters?"

"That's the general opinion."

"Shared by Mrs. Kell. I'm sure my nursing was a matter of a guilty family conscience."

The red-haired girl looked up with a peculiar sidelong glance. "I wouldn't be so sure about that," she murmured. "There's another way to explain it."

She swung away abruptly and went to the post where her rope hung. Within a matter of brief minutes two strong-looking saddle horses were tied to the back of the freight wagon, Jason Applegate helping only after being an interested audience for Miss O'Hara's exhibition of roping.

Finally Quincy went into the store to select the cartons and boxes of food that would complete the freight wagon's load. "We'll roll on up to the spur summit," he told Margaret, "passing the rail crews and their wagons without stopping. By that time I doubt if we'll have too many scouts on our trail. I'll try to get word to Muldoon about our moves but it might be well if you'd make certain that he knows. I want everything in the rail camp to start moving two hours before daybreak tomorrow morning. By the time the stuff reaches the rim above the rock slant we should be ready to start lowering it into the gorge. If we make the move with just the right timing we should catch the enemy off guard."

"Fair enough," she agreed quietly. "I'll make sure that Muldoon gets the order. You'll have a small crew, though. Those wagoners are homestead men who want to get back to their spring planting. As soon as they deliver the stuff they'll pull out."

"I won't need many men. Once we're down into the gorge with the right materials we can lay track as slowly as we please. Length of track is not the important thing right now."

"Suppose they try to rush you?" she suggested.

He shook his head. "This is all supposed to be legal and aboveboard. Their violence will be like the attack on me, something shady and small. I don't think they'll risk any mass attack on Midland property."

She eyed him with a quizzical stare. "For a man who just got a good beating you have a curious amount of confidence in your enemies. You'll be smart to get ready for a real fight."

"Not if I can help it. This is supposed to be a legal battle and I propose to keep it that way as long as I can."

"Too bad," she said, shrugging. "I sent Muldoon a dozen brand new Winchesters and some not-so-bad Springfields in one of the wagons. I suppose you can send them back if you don't want them. Too bad, though; we'd have made a nice profit on that sale."

"We'll keep 'em if we have to use 'em to shoot jack-rabbits," he told her with a grin. "Can't interfere with O'Hara profits. By the way, just take your bill to Pettigrew at the bank. He has orders to pay without any argument. I'll save my cash to pay the teamsters."

He moved away then, fearful that some observer might think he was taking too long with the transaction. He spoke to the girl only once more and then it was to sign a slip which she handed to him.

"We'll not put Pettigrew under any more strain than necessary," she said quietly. "I'll guarantee that your people have received every item listed here. Better for you to take my word for it than Pettigrew."

He signed without even looking at the list. "Suits me," he told her.

They moved north out of Machete, following the same faint trail which Quincy had cut from another angle on his previous trip to the summit of the spur. The wagon was now pretty well loaded but Applegate sent the mules along at a good pace, bellowing at the animals with high good humor and cracking his long whip in a style which marked him as an experienced mule skinner. Quincy watched just long enough to feel sure that his new employee knew his business After that he kept a watchful eye on the back trail, trying to learn how many scouts would come out to trail the wagon.

It didn't take him long to find out. Two riders tailed along about two hundred yards behind the outfit, obviously keeping pace with it. Quincy commented only when they were beginning to start to climb. "We got a pair of sightseers with us," he told the driver. "They don't even take the trouble to hide their intentions."

"That bad?" Applegate inquired, shooting a stream of tobacco juice across the flank of the nearest mule before speaking.

"I don't know. Maybe it's good. We know where they are."

"Let me know if you want me to git rid of them."

"No violence. No shooting," Quincy said shortly. "We don't fight unless the other side forces the fight on us."

"You're the boss."

They went on in silence until they reached the crossing of the old coal siding. Even before they climbed to the ledge on which it ran Quincy could see the results of Muldoon's labors. At least a dozen wagons stood idle along the old roadbed, loaded with ties. Several piles of rail were close to the crossing and other wagons were moving in from both sides with additional material. Apparently crews were at work in two places but Quincy could see neither operation. More important than that he could not see anything of Muldoon.

Because he had no choice in the matter he merely waved

to the workmen as the wagon went through. None of them knew enough of the secret to be trusted with any kind of message to Muldoon and it was no time to stop for talk while those two riders were watching from the rear.

He explained it to Applegate when they were toiling up the grade to the hogback. "Have to depend on the folks in Machete passing the word," he grumbled. "Not that it's too much of a chance. They took mighty good care of the whole deal so far."

Almost before he got the words out he knew that he was wrong about having to depend on Margaret O'Hara. Muldoon himself was coming down the trail toward them. Applegate halted his team at Quincy's order and the Irishman pulled up beside the wagon.

"We had a couple of scouts on our trail," Quincy told him abruptly. "I don't know whether they went back after seeing that we didn't stop at the rail camp or not. If they see us together you can tell them that I was trying to persuade you to sell out to me."

The stocky Irishman grinned. "It's a fine liar I'm making of myself. No reason I can't keep it going."

"Right. Now let's get this over fast. Get every wagon on the road tomorrow morning two full hours before daybreak. If you've got any mules in camp that can be used as pack animals put them into service also. Each mule can carry a rail lashed to its back if you've got men who can do the lashing properly. That's your business; all I care is that we get every possible piece of material on the trail before the opposition knows the move is being made."

"You think they'll try to interfere?"

"Likely. They're watching us mighty close. Did you find any men who know anything about handling block-and-tackle rigs?"

Muldoon grinned. "Jest one. Gossoon named Dutch Fritz. He claims he helped you fight the war."

"Nobody else?"

"Nope. The Dutchman's got another lad up at the rim with him but he's only a helper. Strong back and a weak mind, I'd call it."

"But they're already at the cut?"

"Sure. The lass said as how you'd want things ready for lowering the stuff as soon as it got hauled up to the rim. Fritz is getting the tackle rigged."

"But he's not showing himself up there, is he?" Quincy's words betrayed his anxiety. "We don't want Pacific even to suspect what we're trying to do."

Muldoon chuckled hugely. "Mister, that O'Hara girl has got more smart ideas than a dog has ticks. She sent special orders to Dutchy. He's got to rig his traps under cover till you give him the word."

"I'm more and more convinced that it was lucky I got cracked over the head," Quincy grimaced. "Miss O'Hara seemed to know what I needed before I did."

"She's got a way of doing just that," Muldoon told him. "You'll find the whole shebang right well organized."

"I believe it. Now get along and do some organizing in the rail camp while I go on and find this Dutch Fritz character. He'll need some help if we're going to have that rig ready for operation in the morning. Get the wagons rolling early and keep them coming."

Muldoon threw him a salute and rode on toward the lower slopes.

The freight wagon had climbed another half mile before either of its passengers broke the silence. Then it was Applegate who asked, "Who's this O'Hara woman who's been gettin' so valuable on the deal?"

Quincy chuckled. "You saw her at the livery stable. The redhead."

"Doggone! A real cute li'l gal. How come she's runnin' this here hoe-down?"

"That I don't know. She just seems to have taken charge."

"Sounds like it ain't a bad idea," the Arkansan declared with another wet assault on his favorite mule flank. Even in them dirty pants she looked like a real interestin' female. 'Course havin' brains ain't much good with women but if the gal's got a nice figure and a pretty face a man can manage to overlook the other part."

Quincy didn't even hear him. He was calculating the needs of the next few hours. With no experienced crew to handle the lowering of the rails and ties into the gorge it was going to be a real problem. He just hoped that Dutch Fritz had taught his one helper a few tricks.

Chapter 10

THE TEAM labored slowly up the winding grade, making very poor headway with the heavy wagon in spite of the fact that Quincy was now astride one of the saddle horses, adding his prodding efforts to the mule-skinner talk that Applegate hurled at the animals.

Quincy knew that they were doing well enough for this particular trail but well enough wouldn't do; time was slipping away. Finally he could stand it no longer so he angled in beside Applegate and announced, "I'm going on up. I'll take the other bronc with me. Maybe I can help Fritz with his rigging and it's a cinch I'm not doing you any good here. I don't think anybody will try to interfere with you now."

"Go ahead," the lanky man agreed. "I'll take good care of myself, bein' as how we got some plumb nice guns aboard. Just gimme some landmarks to follow."

Quincy outlined the route as precisely as possible. "Just keeping heading toward that rocky spire when you leave the trail. If you can't find a way through the timber pull up and ride one of the mules on until you find me. Just don't fall into the gulch."

He wondered at his own cheerfulness as he rode forward. With success or failure hanging on the events of the next twenty-four hours he was putting all of his bets on unknown cards. He didn't know enough about Muldoon to be certain that the man would carry out his orders. He didn't know whether Dutch Fritz would be capable of getting the proper rigging into place. He didn't know what materials had been sent up to the rim for that rigging. He didn't know whether Applegate could be trusted to come along. Probably no construction engineer had ever embarked on a big project with less knowledge of his own equipment or crew. Still Quincy felt reasonably hopeful. Anything was better than sitting idly around Machete while the opposition moved

ahead. Maybe his volunteer assistants would prove satisfactory.

He found the riggers working things out the hard way,
two men operating in a stand of piñon close to the rim but
out of sight from the gorge or the opposite side of it. One
was a bandylegged little man whose shoulders and arms
were as big as Quincy's. The other was a hulking youth
who was doing most of the heavy work in stretching out
the big cables. At first Quincy was concerned principally
with that part of the scene. He wondered where they had
located so much rope at short notice.

Then he remembered Dutch Fritz. That gorilla shape
was not too difficult to recall. The man had been a deserter
from a European navy in his early days but had chosen to
join the Union army instead of putting his nautical skill
to use, probably for fear of capture by his old country.
In the hurried business of following up Grant's campaigning forces Schultzenberger had become a name of more
than mere comic value. He had been the non-com who had
handled chores that engineering officers had called impossible, putting up a couple of suspension bridges that were
marvels of ingenuity. Quincy felt better just at sight of the
big shoulders and bowed legs.

Fritz dropped his rope and came over to salute his new
employer, evidently much pleased when he saw that Quincy
remembered him. They spent a couple of minutes in the
usual exchanges between old acquaintances and then
Quincy started to ask questions.

Fritz supplied the answers so rapidly that it was clear
that he had really studied his problem. He even had dimensions, explaining that he had used a simple rig to lower himself into the cut and make some measurements. The break
in the rim was really a series of three rock slides where
rock strata had suffered similar fractures. The first drop
was nearly perpendicular but was only a little over a hundred feet in depth. Then there was a small ledge which
topped a rough, broken slope of perhaps seventy-five degrees which led down another seven hundred feet to a
second and somewhat larger ledge. From that point it was
about four hundred feet to the floor of the canyon, the final
slope being a little less steep and with plenty of irregu-
larities for anchoring rigging. It all sounded pretty formid-
able but Fritz was certain that it could be done. He had

already prepared the slings that would be required for the first and steepest descent.

"Where did you get so much cable?" Quincy wanted to know, eyeing the huge rolls which had been deposited beneath the shaggy trees.

Fritz shrugged. "Muldoon," he said shortly. "He bring me the stuff; I work with it."

Quincy let it go. He had a suspicion that this was more of the canny foresight which had marked all of Margaret O'Hara's arrangements. She had been the first to realize the strategic value of the rim break and it seemed likely that she would have figured on just about everything.

They put in a good two hours' work on their gear, Fritz's helper, a youth named Eddie Morgan, proving to be a lot smarter than he looked. He was strong and he had plenty of nerve, handling the heavy blocks with no show of strain and attending to some preliminary anchorages at the rim as though the sheer drop behind him meant nothing.

The afternoon was well along when the sound of wheels on the sandy soil of the rim interrupted their labors. Quincy motioned for the others to remain quiet while he pushed through the trees to look. He relaxed at once when he spotted the lanky form of Jason Applegate coming toward him, almost dragging the mule team along behind him

"Just bein' careful," the Arkansan explained with a broad grin. "You told me to watch out for the drop and I wasn't figgerin' to lose no mule team down no deep hole."

"See anybody along the trail?"

"Nary a soul. Looks like they didn't follow along after they seen us pass them rail busters."

"We'll hope it was that way. Bring the team on in here by this supply dump. Let 'em rest a while and you scout the place a bit to figure where we ought to make a regular camp. I'll get on with my chores here."

Applegate brought his outfit on in, to be greeted with a raucous shout by Eddie Morgan. "Hiyah, Apple, yuh dadratted hoss thief! When did they let you outa jail?"

The lanky man glared. "Now don't that beat all!" he exclaimed wonderingly. "Here I come way out here so's I could get me among real men and what do I lay my eyeballs on first but a half-wit child. Eddie, does your maw know

you're runnin' around loose without your flannel petticoats?"

Young Morgan ignored the insult, hustling over to shake
hands with the newcomer. Applegate still pretended to be
highly disgusted but he shook hands with the boy in a
manner that marked them as real friends.

"Gimme a hand at unhitchin' these critters," he ordered
gruffly. "It'll get you out from underfoot 'fore you get in
men's way. If a mule tromps on you it won't make no
difference."

Quincy laughed and went on with what he was doing.
He wondered how it had happened that a Muldoon recruit
should appear as an old friend of the Arkansan but didn't
think it worth while to ask questions. Coincidences happened often enough in the West. There was his own meeting with Jeff and Elinor, for example.

Applegate and Morgan took over the business of setting
up camp, continuing with it until just before dusk. Then
Quincy called them over to the rim and the task of putting
the slings into place began. With four of them working they
could get quite a bit done between the beginning of the
operation and the closing down of darkness. Even if they
were observed now it wouldn't make too much difference.

When they knocked off at dark they had their upper
anchorages well set, the rigging dangling down toward the
first ledge. Most of the other gear was already set up, ready
to be lowered into the break at the first peep of day.

"Twelve hours from now we'll be set up—or we'll be
licked," Quincy told the others. "If the timing works out
right—and nobody stops any part of the move—we should
be ready to work when the first load of stuff gets here. After
that we race against time and Pacific."

He didn't sleep much that night. The day's work hadn't
been kind to his aches and pains but his brain was too
active for sore muscles and general weariness to take
charge. The critical hours were just ahead. The one slim
chance of breaking through Pacific's guard was due for a
trial. Maybe he would be able to do the impossible.

He dozed fitfully some time after midnight but was
awake in time to rout the others out for an early breakfast.
At daybreak they were at the rim, beginning the more
tedious parts of the installation. Fritz and Morgan went
down to the first ledge, handling the other gear which

Quincy and Applegate lowered to them. It was hard work for a man who had only recently spent long hours in bed but Quincy didn't complain. He knew that the only way to get the job done was to do it. Other men with less interest were doing yeoman service; he could not do less.

At the first sound of wheels beyond the screen of piñons Applegate went out to direct the teams that were coming in. Quincy sent down the last of the gear and then took over the unloading. The men who were handling the wagons were not going to be regular employees, he understood, so he wanted to let them get on their way as quickly as possible. He might have need for them later so he wanted to keep their good will.

Fortunately the first two drivers turned out to be men who were going to remain with the crew. They took in the situation at a glance and came back to help with the work as soon as they had left their teams at the camp site. After that the unloading went smoothly and efficiently, a pile of ties building as if by magic along the rocky rim. So far no rail had appeared but that was all right. The ties had to go into place first.

Within the hour a shout from below indicated that Fritz and Morgan were ready to handle materials, so Quincy started sending it down. He did not know the names of the men who worked with him but somehow they seemed to take hold and get things going. He knew that Applegate was handling the wagon traffic smoothly enough, so he let the Arkansan alone, concentrating on the work of getting railroad ties lowered into the gorge. One man went down on the slings to help the pair at the first ledge and after that Quincy lost account of time. He even forgot his weariness.

Presently he realized that the rim camp was getting choked with teams and wagons. He stopped work and sought out Applegate. "Don't these men plan to go back for another load?" he asked.

The lanky one shook his head. "Seems like they don't. They're right willing, I understand, but that wasn't the orders."

"Then get them moving. Promise an extra half-day's hire for every team that brings up another load. Plenty of daylight left."

He started away but turned to add, "That makes you a foreman, Jason. Your pay just doubled. Get them rolling!"

"I'll take our wagon down the ridge with the rest," Applegate called, his grin wide. "Seems like somebody down there needs some proddin' about them pack mules."

By the time the camp was clear again it was noon. Quincy halted operations at the rim and brought up the trio from below. They sprawled in the sunshine at the edge of the cliff, disposing of a cold lunch while Quincy explained the operation in some detail. Now that secrecy was ended he wanted his crew to know exactly what the plan called for.

"We've got to get these rails and ties all the way down to the floor of the canyon," he concluded, "or none of this will do a bit of good. A pile of stuff on that first ledge is all well and good but we don't want the opposition there. By now Pacific must know that something big is afoot. If they find out just what it is we're doing they might still have time to push a work party up the gorge and seize the bottom of this rock chute. Then they'd have us blocked instead of us having them."

"I reckon we could get 'em out in a hurry," young Morgan drawled.

Quincy shook his head. "We do it legal. Understand that and remember it. The courts decide that either railroad company had a right to build through the gorge and that neither had a right to interfere with the work of the other. That's why possession of the Keyhole is so vital. If we grab it first the Pacific people will be taking the wrong side of the law if they try to tear up any track we've laid there— and there's scarcely room for one line and certainly no room for two. The first outfit to take possession is in a perfect position."

"How much time before Pacific finds out about this deal?" It was the new man who asked the question, his tones hinting that he might be reasonably well educated. Quincy had learned that his name was Snedaker and that he knew something of railroad construction. The other one, the man who had gone down to help Fritz and Morgan, was named Miranda. Other than that Quincy knew nothing of either.

"I figure Pacific got word of the movement of the wagons about breakfast time this morning. If they weren't too suspicious there's a chance that they took it to be the movement Muldoon has been talking about. If they suspected something they'd have sent scouts up here. Give the scouts an hour to track us down and another hour to get back. Pacific could know of our location right this minute."

"But maybe they don't. Maybe they didn't get suspicious yet."

"They will. When those empties start coming back to be reloaded they'll know. Perhaps we have a couple of hours, perhaps less than that. One way or another we've got to get the first lot of material down into the bottom of the gorge right away. After we get enough stuff down to make a showing we can take our time about moving the rest of it."

After finishing their lunch all five of them went down to the first ledge and proceeded to complete the rigging Fritz and Morgan had already put into partial operation. Within a half hour timbers were going down to the second ledge.

Quincy left Morgan, Miranda and Snedaker to handle the operation. He and Fritz went on with the task of rigging the final drop. It proved to be tedious but not as bad as he had expected. Fritz had made his measurements carefully and had prepared the block-and-tackle gear with those dimensions in mind. At the end of an hour the first slings were in place, ready to test with some of the railroad ties which had come down from the upper ledge.

Quincy made the first trip to the bottom, handling the ties as they came down and placing them so as to block the little shelf of loose rock which formed a narrow rim above the brawling river. The block wasn't really necessary because the rim ceased to exist at the slide. Above that point there were sheer walls of dark rock rising perpendicularly from the swift water to the narrow strip of blue sky overhead. A blockade of ties at this point had no practical value but it would serve as a symbol of Midland's arrival. For the time being Midland held the key to the Keyhole.

It was nearly dark when operations ceased in the rock slide. By that time Quincy had heaved so many railroad ties that his earlier weariness had given way to sheer exhaustion. He had to lash himself into the rigging and have the others haul him back to the rim. It was quite a trip even when a man was at his best and in the gathering gloom Quincy managed to bark his shins several times on the ascent. He collapsed in a heap when they pulled him up to solid rock but he still had life enough in him to grin up at Muldoon. "Looks like we pulled it off," he said. "Everything all right in your bailiwick?"

Muldoon reported at some length. Almost every wagon had made two trips to the rim camp and the mule train was now awaited, being just about due to complete its second haul. There had been no sign of a move from Pacific. Sheriff Naylor and two men had ridden out during the afternoon to watch rails being loaded on the mules but no one had started any trouble. It was beginning to appear that the enemy camp had been caught completely napping, but about five o'clock the men on the rim had spotted two horsemen on the far side of the canyon. Undoubtedly the pair had discovered what was going on.

"How long ago?" Quincy asked. "I'm so tired at this point that I don't know what time it is."

"Five-thirty or thereabouts," Muldoon told him. "Yourself was comin' up outa the hole when we seen the two of them. They'll not get back to Machete before the evening."

"If that's the way of it we're lucky," Quincy told the men around him. "We'll take over the gorge at dawn. If the other side tries to move in they'll be interfering. Not us."

"How close to the cut are they now?" Muldoon inquired.

"A good mile. I couldn't tell for sure because of that big crag they call Rock Corner but anyway they haven't passed it yet. Tomorrow we'll start moving in two directions. We'll grade down toward Rock Corner so as to meet them as far from the Keyhole as possible. At the same time we'll throw a temporary bridge across and begin to grade the easier slope on the far side of the Keyhole, working upstream."

Snedaker stared at him with a quizzical smile showing on his tired features. "Where do we get the crew to do all that?" he asked.

Quincy rolled over, staring about him. The camp was almost deserted. He could see three freight wagons and a lot of tethered mules beyond the piles of ties and rails but the only men in the place were the ones now grouped around him.

"How much crew do we have?" he countered.

Muldoon tallied them for him. "Dutch and his boy you've seen. Likewise Eli and Jules. The tobacco-chewin' character you brought in yourself. That's all there is 'ceptin'

Bally Allen. He's down in the valley standin' guard over the rest of the rails and ties."

"Couldn't you get more? We don't have enough men to do a decent job of grading, let alone to lay rail!"

The Irishman shrugged. "Planting time," he explained. "I could get them to take a day for haulin' but they couldn't afford more'n that."

"What about men from town who aren't farmers?"

"I reckon you know the answer to that one without me telling you. Them as ain't already workin' for Pacific ain't hankerin' to work nohow. You're better off without that kind."

Quincy studied the faces around him. "Maybe so. If these men are game to have a try at it with me we'll see what we can do."

He grinned with satisfaction at the answers he received. It still seemed pretty foolish to be bucking Pacific with a half-dozen men but there was no other way.

Chapter 11

THEY MADE a short evening of it there under the stars on the rim of the canyon. Every man had done more than a good day's work and no one cared to make an occasion of supper. They ate what they wanted wherever they found it, throwing bedrolls in the most comfortable spots and going off to sleep without further ado.

Quincy recovered his stamina long enough to check a few points with Muldoon. For one thing he did not understand why the teamsters had headed for their respective homesteads without waiting for their pay.

"Easy enough," Muldoon chuckled. "The lass had a hunch maybe you'd not be up and about when we done the haulin'. She passed the word that the boys were to call on the O'Haras for their money." He chuckled again as he added, "She's a smart one, is Peggy. It stands to reason if they get their money at O'Hara's they spend some of it there."

"Maybe not so smart," Quincy replied. "It's important all around that we don't let our connection with the O'Haras become known. Pacific's crowd may suspect something but we don't want that suspicion to be any stronger. We might need the kind of help that only an unsuspected ally can give us."

Muldoon rubbed his chin whiskers ruefully. "Looks like we made us a mistake," he muttered.

"My mistake," Quincy contradicted. "I should have kept my wits about me. Instead of trying to handle materials in the canyon I should have been up here checking out the wagoners. How long would it take for you to get in touch with the men who handled this chore for us?"

"Three-four days at the outside. Why?"

"I want every man of them paid in cash. I'm sorry if it seems like I'm busting up a business deal for the O'Haras but that's how it has to be. In the morning I'll provide you with the necessary cash. You'd better hit for town and try to catch any of them who are planning to go in early. Then work through the rest and pay them all off."

"Right. It'll keep me away from this camp fer a spell, you know."

"Can't help it. I want our connection with O'Hara kept quiet as long as possible. While you're riding around the country you'll not be wasted; you can scout a bit and find out what Pacific is planning to do about us. If anybody tries to pump you tell them I offered you more for the rail than you could have got for it up north. Maybe we can keep them in the dark a little longer all around."

Muldoon rode out of camp on one of the new saddle horses a good hour before dawn next morning. Quincy issued orders to the others at the same time, using the grumpy cheerfulness of the early breakfast as an occasion to outline the jobs ahead. Applegate was to take charge of the rim camp. He would receive any new shipments which might come up the ridge. He would serve as commissary, sending food down into the gorge as needed. He would act as guard for the rim camp. He would take care of the animals and the other property still on the rim.

"Sounds like work for a platoon," Quincy told him with a wry grin. "But it won't be as bad as what some of the rest of us will be trying to do. Just handle the most important parts and let the rest go. Use your own judgment all along."

He was happy to get an easy nod from the lanky man. That set a good example for the others. "Snedaker will take charge of track work in the gorge," he went on. "It won't be much, of course, because the only helpers he'll have will be Miranda and part of the time me. Fritz is to start trying his ingenuity out on a rough bridge. We want to throw some sort of span across at the east end of the narrows so that we can start doing some grading in the Keyhole itself. At first all of us will be close together and we can lend a hand from one job to another. For the present we'll consider Eddie to be Fritz's gang but let's not get technical about any of it. I know we've got enough work for a hundred men so I don't expect anything unreasonable. Just keep in mind what we're aiming to do and make the best job possible with the circumstances what they are."

Fritz handled the slings to let the first three men down, Quincy taking the time to inventory the supplies which had been unloaded. He was amazed at what he saw. Not only had the wagons brought in construction material but there was an ample supply of food, shovels, cordage, nails, bolts, canvas, even a couple of cases of dynamite. Someone had done some very smart planning. He had an idea that the planner was Margaret O'Hara but Muldoon had already ridden away so there was no one on hand to support the guess.

Going down on the rigging he couldn't help thinking about the girl. It was beginning to appear that she had been running this show quite as completely as Elinor Kell was handling things for Pacific. And with much less reason. Elinor was actually a majority stockholder in Rocky Mountain Pacific. Margaret O'Hara had no connection with the affairs of the Colorado Midland Company.

A least such had been the case until now, Quincy thought. As of this moment she went on the payroll. Maybe that had been a joke in the past but he determined to list her as a commissary agent or something of the sort. She had well earned any wage which might be paid her.

Fritz followed him to the first ledge, where the other men were waiting. That was a precaution which the rigging boss had ordered on the ground that the ropes had been used roughly on the previous day and should be tested before the men used them. Quincy made it a point to agree. He was trusting men to give him their best work and their best judgment; he wanted them to know that their decisions would be respected.

They inspected the second set of ropes with due care and then Fritz gave the word, the party descending again and waiting until all were down. The third stage was an equally careful proceeding, but soon the five of them were at the base of the slide, five men preparing to start a railroad through an impossible place in order to block the efforts of a construction crew which numbered several hundred. It would have been funny if it had not been so serious.

No one bothered to think about the ridiculousness of it. Snedaker was already staking out a rough level and instructing Miranda in the manner in which to handle it. Quincy paused long enough to say, "Work out the easy parts as far as you can go. Holler for help when you need it but leave us with the bridge job as much as possible."

Snedaker nodded, his grin mirthless. "We'll yell if we need a big one moved. The rest is just a matter of keeping at it. Which is more'n I can say about your bridge chore."

Fritz and Eddie were staring at the turbulent brown flood, both of them looking pretty gloomy. At this point the river was not more than forty feet wide but the compression of its flood waters into that narrow channel had turned it into a mighty violent stream. It fairly exploded as it came out of the Keyhole, a ledge of rocks at that point making the picture all the more wild.

"Any ideas?" Quincy shouted above the roar of the rapids.

Fritz shook his head. "We got timbers for the bridge but I don't see the way to get them across yet."

"How about a suspension bridge for a starter? Then use that to put heavier stuff in place. We don't expect this to be the real thing, you know. It's just a means of getting us across so that we can lay rail in the narrow gorge."

"Ja. That I understood. But with the suspension bridge we got to get ropes across." His shrug indicated that he considered the feat impossible.

Quincy walked upstream until he had no more footing along the base of the sheer cliff. At this point the stream boiled along with a silent fury that suggested depth. This was the spot where the pent up waters were developing their power and speed. At the mouth of the gorge that speed was shattered on the rocks of the shallows. Here a man might swim.

He calculated carefully, estimating the speed of the current and the distance to the far side. It was forty feet to the opposite bank, less than a hundred to the rapids. If a man could swim diagonally into the current and make one-third the speed of the current itself he might get across before the river could dash him on the barrier rocks below the cut. Stated as a mathematical problem it didn't sound so bad.

Then he tried to estimate the flow of water and decided that it wasn't so good either. A man couldn't swim fast enough to get across.

He tried to figure some method of reaching a point farther upstream before making the plunge but there was simply no possibility. Beyond his present position there was no footing whatever.

Fritz edged along beside him, his voice sounding far away as he yelled above the echoes of the gorge. "No good. Water's too swift."

"No other way," Quincy shouted in return. "Track on this side won't make a blockade. We've got to seize a section where two lines of rail can't possibly be placed." He pointed toward a spot just above the rapids. "I think there's a bit of a back eddy over there. If I can get into it before the rocks get me I can make it across."

Fritz shook his head but Quincy ignored him. "Get me a light line that I can tie around my waist. Make it strong enough so you can haul me back by it if I can't make the eddy."

The German shrugged but did not argue. Quincy went back with him to the mouth of the slide, stripping off his clothing while Fritz procured the necessary rope. Then they went back up into the Keyhole, Morgan going along to lend a hand with the rope. That part was going to be tricky enough, Quincy realized. He had to depend on his shore men for plenty of cooperation. They had to let him have just enough slack and still be in a position to haul him clear of the rapids if he missed. There wouldn't be any margin for second guesses.

No one bothered to comment further. Each man knew what he had to do and knew how much risk was involved. Talk would have been no good. Quincy tied the line about his waist and waited until Fritz and Eddie were in position. Then he stepped gingerly into the icy water, trying to gain a yard or two by feeling for any underwater footing which might allow him to go upstream a little farther.

He gained perhaps five feet but then his groping toes could find nothing but perpendicular rock and rushing water ahead. He braced himself briefly and launched himself in a racing dive, angling a little upstream. The lunge gave him a couple of precious yards. The shock of the water was almost numbing but he battled furiously, trying to shake off the possibility of cramps and at the same time gain distance.

He knew that he was being twisted violently by the current but he kept his head down, stroking hard to maintain his headway. Once he felt the rope tangle about a threshing foot but he shook it off and drove ahead. When he looked up he knew that he was a little past midstream but being swept down so rapidly that the white water seemed only a dozen feet away. He twisted a little, fighting the current more directly, and found that he was being pushed sideways toward the opposite bank at a little better rate of speed. He had forgotten the iciness of the water now; all that counted was to get into the eddy before the men behind him had to stop him. He didn't let himself think of the possibility that they might not be able to prevent his being dashed in among those jutting boulders.

A slight tension on the rope told him that they were getting ready to haul in, fearful that the rocks would get him. He knew an instant of unreasoning anger. They couldn't pull him back now! That would ruin everything. He wasted a stroke to wave for more slack and as he did so he could feel a new force to the current. He was being flung directly toward the tiny ledge which marked the lower rim of the south wall.

He put everything he had into a dozen fast strokes and as if by magic the ripping current stopped its struggle. Just above the rapids there was actually a tiny patch of slack water. He exerted another desperate effort and suddenly solid rock was just ahead of him. Even then a final vagary of the current almost snatched his goal away from him but he drove hard, trying to make numb fingers take hold on slippery rocks.

Just as it seemed that he would be swept along the rocky shore into the maelstrom of the rapids he found a crevice that would hold his grasp. He hung there for a few seconds, trying to muster his spent energies, but the numbness struck hard at him and he hauled himself out without quite knowing how he did it.

For a couple of minutes he could not even stand. He was shaking from the strain, the cold, and his recent injuries, but he forced himself to still another effort, quickly gaining a foothold that permitted him to brace himself and take in the slack of his rope.

Coming naked out of icy water into the dank air of the canyon was not much of an improvement. In a gorge where the sun shone only for a few minutes in the middle of the day there could be little warmth in an April morning so he didn't try to find any immediate comfort. He had to keep moving so he clambered along to a spot directly abreast of the rapids, hauling in line all the time. It seemed like years before a heavier rope came across but presently he was able to make the stout line fast to a slab of rock which leaned against the wall.

Fritz promptly pulled the rope tight, fastening it to another stout formation on his side of the river. Almost before it was properly in place Eddie Morgan was coming across, hand over hand, with Quincy's clothes tied to his back. Even that was something of a feat. The line sagged to a point where Morgan splashed in the rapids but he fought his way through, keeping Quincy's garments dry and wetting only his own feet and legs.

The younger man had to do the dressing. By that time Quincy was so numb that he couldn't handle any of his garments. Morgan was rough about it, making something of a massage out of the chore and within a matter of minutes Quincy was able to stamp around in comparative comfort. Still he was content to let the others handle the next stages of the bridge-building. Fritz obviously knew his business and he had plenty of help, Snedaker and Miranda having abandoned their grading work to lend a hand with the bridge.

Fritz came across first, bringing another light line and on that line they brought over tools for making proper anchorages. After that it was routine. A rope ladder was suspended beside the first heavy cable and then other ropes were stretched above it. It took a little time to get everything squared away so that the fastenings were secure on each side of the river, but within an hour and a half they had a sort of rope bridge in place, the ladder serving as a catwalk with the extra ropes as handholds. Now the structure would serve as a base of operations, permitting the crew to place piers at strategic spots in the rapids for the support of timbers. It was going to be a tedious job, Quincy realized, but he knew that Fritz had built other bridges in the past under tougher conditions.

He was still pretty shaky when he went back to the north side of the gorge at noon. Miranda had built a fire of driftwood and they made a small celebration of their noon meal. So far the luck was holding. They had staked a claim to the Keyhole and as yet there had been no opposition. All of them knew that they couldn't hope for a continuation of that latter good fortune but for the time being no one cared. They had done the impossible once; maybe they could do it again.

For Quincy there was another reason to feel pretty good about the morning's work. So far in this campaign he had been letting others do the work for him. Muldoon and the O'Haras had done the planning and the organizing. His men had accepted him but he knew that they must have had their doubts. Now they looked upon him in a new light. He didn't need to worry about their loyalty; their talk as well as their glances assured him on that score.

While they were still resting around the embers of the fire they saw a man coming down through the chute. He was on the middle phase of the trip when Morgan first spotted him, clambering down over the sharp slope with the ropes as guides only.

"Jase Applegate," Morgan anounced. "Seems like he's some flustered. Mostly the old hound dawg ain't got that much jump in his carcass."

Quincy knew a sense of alarm but he tried to hide it by remarking, "I gather that you and Applegate knew each other back home somewhere. Don't tell me that you're old enough to have been in Shelby's outfit with him!"

The younger man grinned. "Nope. I was a Rebel,

though, kinda follerin' the camps after my folks died. Me and Jase got to be real chummy."

Quincy waited but the boy didn't add anything. Maybe it was just as well. The backgrounds of these men were not important.

In the brief silence it was Jules Miranda who cut in smoothly, "I was a Rebel myself. Seems funny now to be working for a Union officer."

For a moment Quincy was worried. Then he thought he understood. These men were opening up to him, showing him a confidence which they had not felt ready to exhibit before. It was a tentative sort of show, he realized, but still it was an overture, perhaps a very important one.

"Pretty odd situation," he agreed with a short laugh. "Fritz and I served in the army in Virginia under Grant. I suppose Fritz had a lot of other commanders before that but I didn't come along until Mr. Lincoln had weeded out the others. Anyway we were both on the Union side. Meanwhile Jules and Jase were fighting our side all the way, probably with some amateur help from Eddie. Muldoon was a Union man. So was O'Hara. Now what difference does it make?"

Snedaker cut in lazily, "Don't count me out. I was in the Union army too. Only difference was I got sent out to Colorado to help with the Injun fightin'. That way I happened to do most of the chasin' instead of gettin' chased all the time."

"Don't put it that way," Quincy warned him with a smile. "You'll have these Rebs thinking they won the war. Our side did plenty of chasing before it was over."

The session broke up in banter that made Quincy feel that he had ironed out the last kinks in his crew. They understood each other now and would work together without difficulties. Unquestionably they would argue on the old subjects but it would not be a personal dispute.

Minutes later he was glad that he had this small consolation. Jason Applegate swung down into the gorge with startling news. Masked men had moved in during the night and had burned all of the remaining tie piles on the lower ridge. Bally Allen, the guard Muldoon had left there as a watchman, had been surprised and tied up, six men doing the work of destruction. Muldoon had found Allen and released him, the pair of them coming back up the rim to report. Pacific had started its counterattack.

Chapter 12

"WHERE'S ALLEN now?" Quincy wanted to know.

"Up on the rim," Applegate replied, gesturing overhead. "Muldoon wanted to get on with his other chore so I left Allen to guard the stuff upstairs. Figured as how you didn't know him personal and it'd be less tangled if I brought you the word."

"Suppose Pacific tries another attack on the rim? This man Allen was caught napping once. We can't afford to lose our supplies."

Applegate took time out to aim a brown spurt at the edge of the river. "I reckon, sir, as how Mister Bally Allen ain't the man to get caught twice in the same snood. The other time he wasn't expectin' no fuss. Now he knows— and now he's got himself a gun. I ain't worried none about Allen."

Quincy smiled in spite of himself. "Sounds like you picked up some quick confidence in the man. Don't tell me we've got another Missouri bushwhacker on our hands!"

The lanky man looked quickly at Morgan as though embarrassed by what he had to report. "Sorry, General, but this time I reckon we wasn't lucky enough to get ourselves a good Confederate. He ain't even a good Yankee. The man talks like a dad-blamed duke or something—but he'll do."

"That's all that matters. Go on and tell me the rest of it. I suppose you've got everything planned out."

"I kinda think the boss has got Jase's number," Eddie Morgan chuckled. "Always showing off!"

"Shut up, young'un!" Applegate snapped. "When you get yourself dry behind the ears you'll maybe have something to show on your own account."

"It's the other end of him that's wet today," Quincy laughed. "But don't bother about that point. If you've got an idea let's have it. Does Muldoon think Pacific will make further attacks?"

"Seems so. If they'd make the break by firing them ties it ain't likely they'll make out to be so damn legal on any other point. I been scouting along the rim while I watched the camp and it 'pears to me that they got two good chances of messin' us up. They could push in some fighting men along this here ledge and they could try to rush the rim camp."

"Go on."

"Ah figure we ought to move them mules up the gulch a piece out of danger. Then we dig us some rifle pits around the camp. One man up there scouts on horseback unless he spots an enemy move. Then he hustles back and gets support from down here to man the lines. Meanwhile we put up some defenses down the canyon a piece in case they try to rush us on this level."

Quincy frowned. "You're talking regular war."

"That's what it amounts to. Ask Allen. Nobody was followin' any law books when they knocked him over the head and tied him up. That wasn't no legal move when they burnt up them ties and piled the rails on the fires to git melted up into tweists!"

Quincy shook his head. "Maybe you've got something. We're already too shorthanded to get our work done, but I suppose we can't take the risk of being overpowered. Remember, though, we aren't hunting a fight. At this point we've gained a good legal advantage. I don't want to forfeit that advantage by getting on the wrong side of the law. We fight if we're forced to fight. Not otherwise."

"Suits me," Applegate declared. "I been shot at often enough so's I ain't gittin' no girlish thrills over the chance to play hero."

"Fair enough. You're defense commander as of right now. Want to get back up to the rim and start this man Allen on patrol?"

"I already got him started," Applegate said calmly. "Since I was in command of that post I took the liberty, sir. For now I'd kinda admire to have a peek at the way she stacks up down the river."

"I'll go with you," Quincy told him. "After the morning I don't think I'd have enough gimp to be any good here but I ought to keep moving around a little." He turned to Fritz and added, "Push the bridge job as much as possible. We're not putting in a permanent bridge, you know. We don't expect it to hold up over another spring freshet. Just get a middle support down on the best bit of rock you can use and tie it up with your long timbers to both sides. Maybe the track we put down will never hold a train but we want track across that bridge and up into the Keyhole on the far side. Anything will do just so it's track."

"Better keep your guns handy," Applegate added. "That south rim looks mighty inviting for enemy snipers."

"Fire if you're fired on," Quincy agreed soberly, "but always remember that we're not out to start any war. We want delay and we want it without bloodshed if we can get it. Our whole game is to hold this pass until the court hands down its decision. We can't risk having another lawsuit undo the work of the one that's now being fought out."

He knew that Applegate wasn't too happy over that repeated demand for peace but he suspected that the Arkansan was making too much of the attack on the tie piles. Jase was not the sort of fellow to be interested in a complicated legal tangle; he knew fighting and was ready to handle his share of it if it should come. Maybe it was just as well.

He was silent as they made their way downstream, following the ledge which would make grading easy on this particular stretch. Newly fallen rocks attested to the erosion of the recent winter but there was still a definite hint that some rough leveling had once taken place along here. He recalled noting that fact when he had ridden up the canyon with Elinor and it puzzled him.

Applegate noticed it also and commented. Quincy shook his head at the lean man's questioning glance. "Hard to tell who did it or why. Maybe Indians. They tell me this was big medicine for the redskin in the old days. One way or another it'll make railroad building easy—if we hold out long enough to get a chance to work on this part of the gorge."

Twice he had to call a halt as weariness overcame him but each time a few minutes of rest permitted him to drive himself on again. Finally they passed the little flat expanse where he and Elinor had reined in their ponies to stare up the gorge at the dark narrows.

"We'll ease around the bend here," he told Applegate. "Might as well have a peek at the Pacific crew before they know we're looking. Never know when you might see something of interest."

He took the lead on the narrower path which edged around Rock Corner, halting abruptly at what he saw. "Looks like I talked too soon," he told Applegate over his shoulder. "They seem to be expecting us."

Coming toward him and not fifty yards away were two horsemen, one of them a stranger but the other Sheriff Ab Naylor. Quincy hesitated for an instant but then pushed forward, getting clear of the bend before Naylor spotted him. He could see the lawman's start of surprise but the fat man did not hesitate even though Applegate had ranged himself at Quincy's side, a Winchester held ready.

By that time Quincy had seen the badge of a deputy on the other man's shirt so he concluded that this first move was to have some color of legality behind it. That was cue enough. He motioned for Applegate to restrain himself, calling out a deliberately jovial greeting.

"Afternoon, Sheriff. I hope you didn't ride all the way out here to tell me that you've caught the thugs who ambushed me. Not necessary, you know. I wouldn't want to keep you out of your chair all these hours for such a small matter."

"Don't be so damned smart!" Naylor bellowed in reply, reining in his horse. "I got a paper to serve on you."

"Then you haven't found my attackers? That's too bad. Probably you haven't caught up with the criminals who burned that old railroad property last night either. Maybe you ought to tend to your lawing a bit more and peddle a few less papers."

"I'll tend to my lawin' in my own way!" the fat man stormed. "And I don't need any sassy talk from no greenhorn. Come here and take this paper. It's a court order."

"Come now, Sheriff," Quincy said soothingly. "Surely a man of your experience doesn't need a sassy greenhorn to tell him that the server of a court order has the duty of delivering into the hands of the person named. You can't make the victim come and get it. Read your book and see."

Naylor's hand dropped toward his gun butt only to halt

in midair as the muzzle of Applegate's Winchester came up. "I didn't come out here to make funny talk with you," the man said with an assumption of dignity. "This is an order from the Court of Elk County. Take it."

He rode forward and thrust it down toward Quincy. Then he whirled his horse on the rough surface of the ledge and pulled away fast.

Quincy laughed. "For a minute I was ready to credit you with a bit of nerve, Sheriff. Then you had to go and spoil it. You'll have me losing all confidence in you."

"Read the order!" Naylor snapped. "I want an answer right away."

"Keep your eyes open," Quincy murmured to Applegate. "I don't think they'll try any tricks but . . ."

He opened the crumpled paper which had been jammed into his hand. It didn't take long to read it even though some legal-sounding phrases had been inserted at points where they tended to obscure the meaning. There was also enough bad grammar to make him think that this had been the work of Judge Potter at some moment when the jurist was only slightly inebriated. It was in the general form of an injunction and it ordered one John Adams Quincy, the Colorado Midland Railroad, all employees of said railroad, and any other persons now connected with the operations of said railroad to cease and desist from trespassing upon certain rights of way owned by certain citizens of Machete, Elk County, Colorado, said rights of way consisting of an established wagon road through Devil's Canyon. The owners of the road were named as Jeremiah Winters and others.

He read it aloud to Applegate after digesting it for himself. Then he looked up at the waiting lawmen. "You and the judge ought to get somebody else to write your papers, Naylor," he said. "This one's full of mistakes."

"That ain't neither here nor there! It's a legal court order. I'm warnin' you to pay heed to it."

"Sorry, Naylor. I reckon my answer will have to be a refusal. This so-called road hasn't been in repair for a long time, as anyone can see. It doesn't go anywhere so it's not a true thoroughfare. If it's anything it's public domain and not the private property of Winters or any other crook."

"Don't be blackguarding honest citizens!" Naylor shouted. "The law's the law and I'm here to enforce it."

"Stop making jokes, Sheriff," Quincy said with a shake of his head. "The only law you enforce is the kind you and Jeff Kell cook up between you—with a bit of advice from a drunken judge. I think you know who slugged me and who set fire to our ties. Maybe you even ordered both moves. You're a fraud and you know it!"

The fat man's red jowls fairly quivered with anger. "I ain't takin' that kind of talk from nobody!" he howled. "I put a court order in your hand and I'll enforce it if I have to swear in a whole damned army of deputies!"

"Hired by Pacific, no doubt. But remember this is going to be mighty hard to explain when Midland lawyers start an investigation of the improper handling of your office."

Naylor shot another uneasy glance at Applegate's rifle, steadying himself with a visible effort before lowering his voice so that it almost matched that of his tormenter. "What Midland lawyers?" he finally managed to rasp. "Ain't going to be no lawyers ever hear about this, mister. You'll just be another outlaw what got killed resistin' the law. How do you like that?"

He spurred his horse down the gorge without permitting Quincy to offer a reply. His deputy followed and Quincy watched them in silence for a full minute, considering the meaning of that last threat. It was Applegate who broke the tension by asking, "Still reckon they'll play legal? I'm guessin' we'd oughta build a rock breastwork here back of Rock Corner. A couple of men could hold it real good. Enemy couldn't git around the big rock more'n one or two at a time."

"But it's not this stretch we need to defend."

"Mebbe not. But this is a damn fine outpost for the real defense. If we start delayin' 'em here we can keep men out of the line of fire up the gulch. By the time we fall back to the real line we can make it real nasty for them—and maybe save the time you need."

Quincy laughed. "I shouldn't have argued. Any man who spent the war with Shelby knows all there is to know about retreating actions."

Applegate didn't even blink. "You ain' just talkin', mister. Our boys made a couple of raids but mostly we fought the war between two armies, ours and the Yank outfit that was chasin' them."

"I understand," Quincy assured him. "I wasn't trying to

be funny with that remark. In our armies it was generally
conceded that if the Confederate command had placed
Shelby in command of an army instead of wasting him on
the chore of saving inferior generals from their own stu-
pidity we'd have had a lot more trouble west of the Mis-
sissippi."

"We ain't goin' to fight about that point," Applegate
vowed. "It's sure the truth. Want me to stay here and build
me some breastworks?"

"If you think your man on the rim is all right without
you."

"He'll get along."

"Then use your own judgment. You're in charge of defense plans. I wasn't making jokes when I said that either."

He walked back up the gorge alone, trying to figure out
what the enemy plans would involve. If desperation should
cause Pacific to mount a full-scale attack, either without
the sheriff or with him, it would be a mighty desperate affair
for the handful of men in the gorge. The defense position
was strong but it was not well concentrated. Attacks might
be launched from either rim or from the lower gorge. It
needed three defense forces.

He was not feeling particularly happy over the situation
when he reached the foot of the slide. For the moment he
held the strategic narrows—and he had got some malicious
pleasure out of baiting Sheriff Naylor—but there was no
point in ignoring the deadly possibilities. With a half-dozen
men he had to hold his position against whatever forces
the local law and the Rocky Mountain Pacific Railroad could hurl against him. He had struggled to get a
good legal position but now it was becoming apparent that
the enemy was prepared to abandon the legalities of the
fight.

He rested a while, mostly because he didn't have enough
energy left to do otherwise, then took a hand with the
bridge-building. Fritz and his skeleton crew had already
anchored a piling on a rocky ledge in midstream, running
a stringer to it from the shore. Quincy helped them to put
up the necessary braces and by that time it was getting too
dark to work. Dusk came down early when a man had to
work at the bottom of a hole nearly a quarter of a mile
deep.

It had been a good day's work, he knew. The worst part

of putting up a bridge was in getting it properly anchored. That was done. On the morrow work would move along more rapidly.

He did not need to tell the others about the meeting with the sheriff. Applegate came in just as the crew quit for the day, describing the interview in delighted although somewhat exaggerated terms. There didn't seem to be any doubt about the sentiments of the newly recruited Midland men. They seemed to be getting a vast enjoyment out of Naylor's anger.

"Don't crow, men," Quincy warned them. "I'm afraid I just made him madder than ever. He'll risk something extra to get even."

"Let him come," Snedaker growled. "We'll twist his tail some more."

"I'm serious," Quincy persisted. "Our object is to get a job done, not to annoy even a crook like Sheriff Naylor. I'm afraid we can't hope to outfight him indefinitely; we're too badly outnumbered. We've got to outsmart him."

"You talk like he's the boss man now," Applegate cut in. "Ain't he just fronting for Pacific?"

"I suppose so, but we're trying to make this legal. For the moment he represents whatever law they have in these parts. He's our main foe."

"Sounds funny when you say it that way but I reckon you got it right."

"You got something in mind?" Snedaker asked.

"A vague idea. I don't believe they'll try anything very rough without sounding us out first. Tomorrow there may be some small moves on the part of the opposition but I don't think it will be a serious attempt to dislodge us. For that reason I think it's safe for me to leave here and make a trip into town."

"Trying to get beat up again?" Applegate asked dryly.

"It could happen, I suppose, but now I'll be on guard. I simply want to nail down our legal position. If it'll cramp the enemy's style it needs doing."

"Going in alone?"

"Yes. We can't afford to weaken the defenses here. Maybe I can even recruit an extra man or two to bring back."

"We can sure use them," Miranda stated, speaking for all of them. "But if you can't find them don't worry. We'll make out."

Chapter 13

QUINCY WAS pretty lame when he awakened next morning. Sleeping in the damp depths of the canyon hadn't done much for sore muscles and half-healed bruises but he didn't think that he was any the worse for his icy bath of the previous day. He issued instructions for the work that was to be carried on in his absence, helped with the breakfast, and generally loosened up in the process. When he started the ascent of the rock chute he felt better than at any time since the assault.

Fritz insisted on sending him up the easy way, using the rigging to haul him to the upper levels instead of letting him make the climb on his own. It took two men from the canyon work but it was probably worth it, so Quincy did not argue. He had a long day ahead of him and there was no sense in wearing himself out before it even started.

At the rim he paused to pass a few words with the round, genial-looking fellow who stood guard there. "You're Allen, I suppose?" he greeted.

The chubby man bowed formally. "Balfour Allen, at your service, sir," he said. "I take it you are Mr. Quincy."

"You can drop the mister. Any sign of trouble around?"

"Not an inkling. I patroled the scrub for a half-mile in all directions immediately after the dawning but saw no sign of the misbegotten wretches who are supposed to be threatening us."

Quincy smiled. "You're a bit British, aren't you?" he asked, doing a small imitation of Allen's accent.

"British as all hell," the other agreed cheerfully. "Your friend Muldoon calls me Lord Bilgewater. I've been called lots worse, mainly by my relatives."

Quincy told him of the situation on the lower level. "Keep an eye out for any surprise moves. They might try to burn out this camp as they burned out the tie piles."

"You're blaming me for that?" Allen asked quietly.

"No. But I'll blame you if it happens again."

"It won't."

"That's all I want to know."

"Maybe you might want to know something else. I can name two of the incendiarists."

"You can?"

"Of course. I don't believe they particularly cared about concealing their identities. A certain defiance, I suppose it was. One was a Pacific construction man named Devlin. Another was a town rowdy by the name of Matt Ames."

"I might have known. Is Ames the short, stocky fellow with a bundle of hay on his face?"

Allen smiled faintly. "No. There was a man in the group who fitted that description but I did not know his name. Ames is a tall man, almost as tall as yourself but much more slightly built, particularly across the shoulders. Big jaw and a nasty voice."

"The burly one is Jerry Winters," Quincy told him. "Thanks for the information. Maybe I can use it in my business today."

He went on to explain his general plans. "Likely I'll be coming back in the dark so don't mistake me for Ames. I don't like playing tag with bullets. And you might also keep an eye out for Muldoon. He could be coming into camp late today. If he does you'd better keep him up here until I return."

It was a little past noon when Quincy rode into Machete, well aware that he had been under surveillance since coming out into the open on the lower slope of the ridge. There had been no sign of Pacific scouts on the ridge itself but the town was full of armed men, most of them in the saddle or with their horses tied nearby. Some sort of operation was in process of getting started.

He went directly to the little frame house beside the brick jail. Six horses were at the hitch rack in front of the place so he was not surprised to find the sheriff's office crowded. He went in without knocking, finding himself between two grim trios with the sheriff sitting behind the desk. Evidently the scouts had informed Naylor of his approach and this was the reception committee. Quincy noted that every man in the room except Naylor himself was a stranger but that each wore a deputy's badge.

"The Law—in force," he commented, looking around him. "Really an honor, I'm sure."

"No smart stuff now!" Naylor warned.

Quincy bowed. "You wrong me, Sheriff. I came to lodge a complaint with you as the principal arm of the law. The other day I made a deal with a man named Muldoon whereby I purchased from him certain quantities of used railroad material. After part of the property had been removed at my orders the balance of it was destroyed by arsonists who attacked and bound my watchman. I have information that three of the criminals who committed this combination of arson, assault, and battery were named Jeremiah Winters, Matt Ames, and Something-or-other Devlin. I wish to swear out a warrant for the arrest of those three men and any John Does who accompanied them."

"You got any proof?" Naylor asked sarcastically.

"Enough." Quincy told him. "But that's not your affair. You don't examine my witnesses; you just carry out your own job."

"Look here, mister! I ain't havin' no cocky greenhorn come into my office and tell me what my job is."

"Maybe you should," Quincy replied calmly. "A public official who fails to carry out his sworn duty is subject to certain penalties. So far you've failed to do anything about two separate attacks upon me personally. In this case I can name the criminals. I've done so. Do I understand that you still refuse to do your duty?"

Naylor almost exploded. "You get out of my office!" he bawled.

Quincy nodded casually to the six grim-eyed men around him. "Remember that, boys," he advised. "The next sheriff might be somebody who's a deputy now. It would be real convenient for some ambitious lad to bear witness to the non-feasance of the present incumbent."

That held them for a moment or two. Quincy was out on the street again before they quite recovered from fancy language. He even grinned a little as he turned his back on the sheriff's office and moved up the street toward the bank. He could only hope that his remark might have sown some seeds of distrust in the enemy ranks.

At the bank he gave Pettigrew a brief summary of his situation and plans, asking that the story be transmitted to Midland headquarters as swiftly as possible. It would have to be mail, of course, since the telegraph line was a Pacific monopoly. Then he replaced the cash money that had been used for paying the wagoners. Only when he was ready to leave did he ask the banker about the injunction Naylor had attempted to serve.

Pettigrew grimaced. "I heard about it although they've been keeping it mighty quiet in town. There was a sort of prospect trail up through the cut some years ago. That's what they're using as an excuse."

"Not a real road?"

"No. But the claim could tie things up while courts decided. Meanwhile they must plan to get around you some other way."

"Obviously. Naylor made it plain that he proposes to wipe me out, using his legal position as a cover. That's why I felt safe in coming into town today. He doesn't want to arrest me; he wants to get rid of me in a manner that will keep me from doing any talking."

"I can't believe that he would dare."

"You'd better believe it. Heard anything from Denver about that lease?"

"Not a word. Naylor and Kell are putting a censorship on the news, I imagine."

"Likely. They can't afford to let news in or out."

He went out again, making the rounds of several stores as a blind for a visit to O'Hara's. He didn't notice any great cordiality anywhere, but he had a feeling that people were viewing him a little more tolerantly. Maybe Naylor's hold on the town was slipping a bit.

At O'Hara's he found Margaret alone in the store. "I came to buy a jacket against the cold of the canyon—in case anybody comes in to snoop," he told her quickly. "Meanwhile my thanks for the smart planning you've been doing. In case the store doesn't make as big a profit as it should from the deal I've put you on our payroll as a supply foreman. If anything happens to me present your bill to Pettigrew."

"Thank you, sir. You didn't seem to think so highly of my planning when last we spoke. Too many guns, you hinted."

"I've changed my mind. Now we need men for the guns."

She raised her voice a little. "Will you step over this way, sir? I'm sure we have just what you need."

He followed her without turning around, well aware that she was talking for the benefit of someone who had just entered. For the next couple of minutes he concentrated on the purchase of a sort of blanket coat which she took from a rack, eventually letting his glance pass over a man who had come in to lounge near the hardware counter.

Margaret took the initiative when the coat deal was about complete. "Now the gun," she said briskly. "We still stand ready to make you the loan we promised that day when Sheriff Naylor was with you—or I'll sell you a good Officers Model Colt with gunbelt and a supply of cartridges. It is as you choose."

"I'll buy," he told her shortly. It was hard to sound so curt when he wanted to show her that he appreciated the hint she was passing so cleverly. Still he had to play the game for the spy who was watching him.

He saw her stiffen as she handed him the weapon and this time he glanced around quickly. Elinor Kell had entered the store and was coming directly toward him, tense worry reflected in both eyes and voice as she exclaimed, "I've got to talk to you, Jack. Will you come with me?"

"Better talk here," Quincy said after a moment of hesitation. "I've got to be getting back to camp." He realized that the Pacific man was edging toward the door.

Elinor shook her head, paying no attention to anyone in sight but Quincy. "I wish to speak with you privately," she insisted.

The front door slammed as the Pacific man departed hurriedly. Miss O'Hara took a quick cue. "I'll be movin' back into the house," she announced, assuming her thick brogue—for what purpose Quincy couldn't guess. "You'll be alone here till another customer comes along. Maybe you can make it do."

Elinor tried to smile. "Thank you, Miss. You're very kind."

Margaret disappeared quickly and the dark-haired woman spoke almost without waiting for her to go. "Things have changed, Jack. I'm afraid of what I see, and I can't do anything about it. They'll try to force you out of the canyon, using guns if necessary."

He had wondered for a moment whether she might not

be playing a part, trying to scare him into a move that her company wanted but now he felt sure that she was sincere —and scared.

"The last I knew you were the boss," he reminded her. "What happened?"

"Several things. I had a majority control of the stock of Rocky Mountain Pacific but I didn't own it. I held proxies from a lot of other stockholders. Yesterday I discovered that there have been some deals behind my back. I'm not in a position to call the turns any longer. A new general manager has been appointed and he arrived in town last evening. He is backing Jeff all the way in some sort of plan to force a passage of Devil's Canyon."

"And what happened to all of this fine talk about keeping everything legal?"

"I don't know."

"I do. Pacific was hot for the legal position while it gave them an advantage. I played it according to their rules, so now they want to change the rules."

She nodded, not meeting his eye. "It's no game any more," she said. "They've organized what they call a Machete Citizens' Committee and they are making a lot of loud talk about protecting the rights of the community against Midland's seizure of public property. I'm afraid it's just a blind to hide the fact that the local law has been bought out by my company. And the local law is hiring deputy sheriffs who are no more than gunmen. I can't stop it but I had to tell you about it. Please take care of yourself."

"Thanks," he said dryly. "That's what I'm planning to do. That's why I just bought a gun. Now you'd better get out of here in a hurry. That man who left when you came in is one of the hired guns you mention. Undoubtedly he hustled out of here to report several things, one of them being the fact that you came to warn me."

"I don't care about that. Jeff and I are through. He has shown himself to be such a scoundrel that I want nothing more to do with him."

"Then you have strengthened your suspicion that he was to blame for the attack on me?"

"How did you know . . . ?"

"That you suspected? It was easy. Almost as easy as figuring that he ordered me slugged. I don't think I needed too much warning after that, but thanks for your effort any way."

"Let me add one thing. Armed men have been gathering ever since you arrived in town. I'm afraid they won't let you leave."

"I'll be on guard," he told her quietly. "Now get out of here before Jeff gets jealous again and starts another brawl. I suppose you realize that the first outbreak was probably caused that way?"

This time she looked up. "I thought so," she murmured. "I'm afraid he had good reason—if my feelings are what count."

She practically fled out of the store then. Quincy watched until she had disappeared from view. Then he turned to pick up the new revolver and load five of its chambers, first testing its action while it was empty. As he picked up the belt to fasten it around his waist he spoke in his normal voice.

"You can come out from behind that rack, Peggy O'Hara. The next time you pretend to leave a place by simply closing a door you'd better not make so much rustle after you're supposed to be outside. Maybe the next person you aim to fool won't be so excited as Mrs. Kell was. They might notice."

Margaret O'Hara stepped out at once, more concerned than embarrassed at being caught. "I didn't know you and Mrs. Kell were so well acquainted," she said wonderingly.

"I almost married her," he replied. "That was almost eleven years ago."

"Then you still trust her?"

"I believe in her warning, if that's what you mean."

"Do you think they'll try to prevent your departure?"

"Hard to tell but I doubt it. When they lose their interest in being legal they like to do it under cover. For the moment I'm fairly safe in town—while it's daylight. That's one reason why I want to get on the trail without delay. Thanks for the neatly concealed advice about carrying the gun. The Pacific lad was completely fooled, I think."

"I'll try to send you more men," she promised.

"Then be mighty careful about it. I don't want you or your folks exposed to any retaliation. You're the only friends I've got."

"You forget Mrs. Kell. She's a very pretty woman."

"So I've been told. I've also been told that Gavin O'Hara's redheaded daughter is a real cute lass. I didn't need either bit of information, having eyes in my head."

"Now you're talking nonsense."

"Just as you were when you mentioned Mrs. Kell's charm. At the moment there's no time for the appreciation of the prettier things in life. They'll keep until later."

He pulled out his wallet. "Now let's get down to business. How much is my bill?"

She figured on a piece of wrapping paper, overcharging on every item and then adding the total wrongly so as to give the house another ten-dollar break. Quincy paid without murmur. Only when he was halfway to the door did he turn and grin at the now somewhat disturbed young woman.

"Call that a down payment on your wages as general agent—and don't think I went blind because you were trying to look prettier than usual. Like I said, I've got eyes in my head and they're pretty good eyes for all kinds of figures."

He wondered at himself as he went out. It had been a lot of years since he had talked like that to a girl. Somehow it was still fun.

Chapter 14

BECAUSE THE afternoon was warm he draped the new coat across the horn of the saddle. At least that was what he told himself was the reason. It was not too convincing a thought because he knew quite well that he had to be on the lookout for trouble. It was just as well not to have the tails of the jacket covering the new gun.

He mounted calmly enough, making a show of being very deliberate in every movement. It gave him a chance to look around and at the same time forced him to keep his mind on his immediate future instead of chuckling over his recent words with Margaret O'Hara. What he needed to keep in mind was the girl's warning, not her play-acting or her crazy stunt of overcharging him.

He rode around past the O'Hara livery stable, waving a casual hand at the Irishman who came to the door. If anyone happened to be watching they would not have suspected that there was anything more than the merest of acquaintances between the two. The back end of Machete was as clear of enemies as the street had been. Which was odd. A half-hour earlier there had been a lot of armed men in town.

Quincy started toward the old northeast trail but changed his mind almost immediately when he realized that the enemy forces had disappeared. He knew that the word from the man who had been in O'Hara's store must have had something to do with this mass disappearance. Maybe they were planning to ambush him somewhere along the trail.

He studied the ground as he rode along the base of the Elk spur, finding no unusual quantity of sign. There were the marks left by himself and a few other single riders but no marks of any group. He moved on toward the river, following much the same course he had taken on that first trip into the canyon. Just as he was approaching the strip of timber he saw what he was looking for. Some fifteen or twenty horsemen had passed here very recently, riding hard toward the lower slopes of the Elks.

He followed the trail at once. It crossed the old roadbed of the coal siding but did not follow it. Quincy was a little disappointed. He had half-expected that the riders would have used that path as a hidden detour. Instead they had moved straight up the main slope of the Elks, almost in the angle where the spur extended out from the main part of the ridge.

At first he thought he should follow them because he fully expected that they were making a short cut toward the camp on the rim. Then he changed his mind. This was strange country to him and there would be a lot of risk in tailing such a substantial force of the enemy. Maybe they even had planned the move to induce him to make such an error.

"Better stick to the trail I know," he muttered. "It's longer but it ought to be somewhat easier. Maybe I can even beat them to the camp and pass the word."

He pulled back to the roadbed, letting his horse run

while they were on the easy grade of the old siding. When they struck the main climb up the northern slope he eased the pace, saving the mount as much as possible.

The first haze of dusk was beginning to filter down among the piñons when he reached the summit of the pass and broke away from the trail toward the rim camp. There had been nothing to indicate that anyone had preceded him along the trail so he was beginning to scoff at his own precautions. Pacific was probably up to something but for the moment it didn't involve him.

He had just crossed the bit of open rock country when he heard the distant crackle of gunfire. At first there were three well-spaced shots, then a series of explosions from a somewhat nearer point. He pulled up for a moment or two, listening as the exchange continued. Judging from the sound, it was a three-cornered skirmish with one of the parties on the far side of the canyon rim. At a guess he made it two parties of Pacific snipers banging away at the rim camp from two separate positions, Allen offering an occasional shot in reply.

He sent the horse forward at a run, ignoring the way the stunted pines were tearing at his legs. This might be just a piece of calculated annoyance on the part of Pacific but it might be the opening of an attack on the rim camp. Allen should have help.

He was within two hundred yards of the camp when two men drove their horses directly into his path. They had raced to intercept him, he realized, and the interception was not going to be a peaceful one. Both had guns in their hands. Because he was facing the sunset he could not tell anything more about either man.

Nor was there any time for such study. One of them blasted a shot at him at once, the other holding his fire until he could drag his horse to a halt. By that time Quincy was moving to his own defense. He swerved his pony sharply, passing to the right of the men as they fired at him. For a moment he thought he might break through without a real showdown but the pony swerved again, refusing to plunge into a thicket that was directly in his path. The move kept Quincy in the line of fire and for a moment there was a rapid exchange of lead, no damage being done on either side.

By that time the two enemies were closing in again and

now Quincy saw that one of them was Matt Ames. The lanky man was hunched over his horse's neck so as to be almost concealed, but that lantern jaw was unmistakable. The other man was a stranger but Quincy fired at him first for the very good reason that he was leading the attack.

The shot brought a howl of pain and the man slid from the saddle to roll in the dust until the trunk of a tree stopped him. By that time Quincy was changing the tide of battle, attacking now instead of defending himself. He figured that he had just one cartridge left in the gun, so he saved it for a shot at close quarters, driving in at Ames.

The lanky man didn't seem to like the idea. He fired, seemed to be having trouble with his gun, and then turned tail, ducking out of sight into the timber without Quincy ever pulling the trigger. Quincy followed him a few yards but then turned to go back to the scene of the fight.

He was just in time to see a limp figure riding away. Apparently the fallen man had not been too badly hurt. Given a few minutes' respite he had captured his horse and made his escape. Quincy was just as well pleased to have it so. A prisoner, especially a wounded one, might be an embarrassment. Certainly there would be no point in making any charges against the man. Not while Ab Naylor was running Machete's law.

Halting at the spot where the man had fallen he looked for sign, at the same time listening to the sporadic firing which still sounded from the rim. Allen seemed to be the only one doing any shooting from this side now. He was letting go with an occasional shot but the gunmen on the far side were continuing to make it a rather brisk affair. Quincy didn't quite see why.

He traced the spots of blood on the ground and found where his enemy had recovered his footing. Then he saw the gun, evidently where it had been dropped by the wounded man. In the gathering twilight he did not notice anything unusual about it but something about its feel in his palm made him take notice. He holstered his own weapon and turned the captured one over in his hands. It was the Prescott he had picked up on the depot platform after that first brush with Machete's welcoming committee. It had the notches that he had noticed.

"Looks like Naylor's really after me. Now he even arms

his gang with guns that were left with him as evidence. Can't be he's expectin' to make it sound very legal." The words came out half-aloud and Quincy caught himself up as he heard his own voice. It was no time for that kind of idiocy. He had to get on to the rim camp and see what this was all about.

He put the captured Navy revolver in a saddlebag and reloaded his own weapon. Then he rode on cautiously, aware that all of the firing had ceased now. Dusk was rapidly turning into night and it seemed likely that the shooting had ceased because men could not locate their targets any longer.

He held himself alert for another ambush but was still caught napping when a harsh voice commanded, "Up with the hands, my friend! My gun is aimed squarely at your guts. Make it fast!"

Quincy's start was quickly replaced by a nervous chuckle. It was almost humorous to hear the cultivated accent of Mr. Balfour Allen trying to sound tough. At least it would have been funny if Mr. Allen hadn't developed a small reputation for being tougher than he ever tried to sound.

"Quincy here," the tall man announced hastily. "Are you expecting company?"

Allen's voice sounded relieved as he replied, "They've been all around. I didn't know what they might try next. Ride on past me and you'll find the wagon. Better keep your gun ready until we ascertain where the enemy is now located."

Quincy followed directions and presently he was talking in whispers to Bally Allen, getting the guard's account of the twilight skirmish. It appeared that a half-dozen riflemen on the far side of the canyon had started a peppering fire which had been intended to cover the approach of other men on the near side. Fortunately Allen had not been in camp when the firing began. He had been doing some patroling at a little distance and had intercepted the first party of attackers. There had been a bit of hasty firing as he fell back toward the rim camp but no one had followed him, perhaps because they were afraid the camp was guarded by several men. The long-range fire, of course, had meant little or nothing. A couple of the wagons had bullet holes in them but none of the stock had been hit.

"There was some right smart firing back in the timber," Allen added quietly when he had finished his own account. "I didn't have anything to do with it. Maybe you already know."

Quincy nodded. "Couple of 'em tried to ambush me. I winged one and picked up his gun. Souvenir."

He said no more about it, being more concerned about the meaning of the major attack. It was possible that the whole movement had been contrived as a cover for the attack upon himself but he still couldn't assume it to be the case. He had to prepare for further trouble.

They made supper, a makeshift meal, one cooking while the other one walked a picket line at a distance from the camp. No one stirred in the pines and no shots were fired from across the gulch. Then they traded places and the result was the same. It seemed that the first skirmish was over.

Muldoon came in just before they finished the relay supper, his approach challenged by Quincy, who was on guard at the time. He had nothing of importance to tell, his news from Machete a little older than Quincy's. He did have a promise of two more recruits to come the next day, men who had decided to drop their farm-laborer jobs in favor of better-paying assignments with Midland.

"We'll use them," Quincy told him. "The main thing right now is that we take only men we can trust. We'll have to be careful that Pacific doesn't plant their men in our camp."

"This pair's all to the mustard," Muldoon promised.

The night passed without incident and at dawn Allen went out to scout the ridge summit while Quincy descended to the canyon floor. Muldoon would handle affairs on the rim until further notice, being on hand there to help Allen with possible defenses as well as to meet any recruits who might turn up.

In the gorge he found matters a little more advanced than when he had left. The bridge across the Boulder was now worthy of the name, heavy stringers spanning the turbulent stream and now in process of being locked into position by a dry masonry wall on either end. Such abutments would not last through a winter and spring, everyone knew, but neither would such a bridge. Its only purpose would be to permit track building on the south side of the Keyhole and Quincy thought it would do that very well.

Applegate reported that he had exchanged shots with a rifleman on the south rim at about noon on the previous day but the shooting had been little more than a gesture of defiance on either side. At about twelve hundred feet accuracy was not likely to be great, no matter whether the range was horizontal or vertical.

"It's a point we'll have to remember though," Quincy commented. "If they really put their minds to the business of breaking in on us they'll probably use a cover fire from the rim. A nice rock wall like you've built down the gorge won't be much good against bullets coming straight down."

Applegate grinned. "That's a chore fer the fellers on the rim. They got to keep that dang rim clear of snipers."

"But it's quite a chore to guard the camp. Only one man on the job until today. Even if we get a few more recruits we ought to have them down here."

"Ah reckon so. But seems as if we ain't needin' to stand guard over so much of a camp. How about movin' the wagons and the mules up the gorge a mile or so? It ain't likely them Pacific gunnies is going to nose around that part of the woods. If the men on the rim can be free to scout around they'll keep things right clear, I'm thinkin'."

"We'll try it," Quincy promised. "I'll try to give you an extra man here if we get enough extra recruits. Sounds like we might pick up three or four."

"Don't fuss none about me. I'm doin' real good."

"How's the enemy moving with their roadbed work?"

"Fair. They ought to be smack-dab up against the big rock by late afternoon today.

"Any indication of what they're planning to do then?"

"Nothin' I've spotted."

"Keep your eye peeled. I'll be with the bridge crew most of the time today. If you need help I imagine a shot will be heard above the roar of the river."

Applegate spat lazily at the nearest rock. "You figure we're gonna get jumped?" he inquired.

"Looks like it. Naylor has been assembling a lot of gunmen in Machete, putting deputy's badges on them. Yesterday they left town while I was still there and they headed up this way. Only a few were involved in that shooting yesterday afternoon, so we've got to believe that the rest are staying out of sight, ready to move in when they get the signal. It might happen on this level."

He went back to the new bridge, lending a hand with the final touches on the abutments while Snedaker and Miranda started to rough-grade the south bank of the gorge. The bridge crossed the Boulder at too sharp an angle for a rail line to be curved across on it but no one cared very much about that. The real rail bridge would have to be constructed later. For the present the only concern was to have a way of carrying materials across so that a road-bed could be driven into the Keyhole. Even a little bit of track in that narrow stretch would give Midland the legal foothold it needed.

Shortly after noon they began to carry ties and rails across, the whole crew taking a hand at grading and then placing the rail. It was not a very efficient way of building track but within an hour there was about fifty feet of it down, track being spiked down as fast as roadbed could be leveled for it. It wasn't much, but for the first time Quincy felt that he had really accomplished something. Midland had taken possession of ground it was legally entitled to hold, ground that was now inaccessible to Pacific in any but a completely illegal move. To take possession now Pacific would have to break the law openly.

He was still keeping the men at the track-laying chore when a gunshot cracked faintly above the roar of the river. Eddie Morgan pointed downstream. "Jase's got a bee in his bonnet. Lookit him wave!"

Quincy saw the blue haze of smoke above Applegate's little fort. The Arkansan was gesturing violently, pausing between waves to point toward Rock Corner. Evidently his signal had been occasioned by something that was happening around the bend.

"Morgan and Miranda!" Quincy shouted. "Get rifles and come with me. At the double!" He was running as he yelled, crossing the bridge at full speed but slowing to a more reasonable pace when he began to make his way along the rocky surface of the north-side ledge.

He had covered perhaps a hundred yards, when Applegate fired again. This time Quincy saw what had happened. A man carrying a rifle had come into view around Rock Corner and Applegate had driven him back with a slug placed well up on the wall over the fellow's head. The expected move by Pacific seemed to be developing.

Chapter 15

QUINCY SLOWED his pace when he saw that Applegate had matters under control, letting the other pair overtake him.

"What do you figure it means?" Morgan panted as they closed in on the rock fort.

"Hard to tell. We'll let Jase tell us."

Before they could reach him, however, a pole bearing a white rag was thrust around the corner of the crag. It was followed, after a cautious interval, by an unarmed man. Quincy recognized him at once as the nondescript fellow who had shadowed him in Machete.

The man with the flag of truce came on steadily toward Quincy, keeping his glance carefully away from the three Midland riflemen. At a distance of perhaps thirty feet he halted and pointed to the badge which appeared on his shirt.

"I'm a deputy sheriff and I've got a warrant for the arrest of John Adams Quincy. I could also arrest the man who just shot at me but it'll be easier all around if Quincy will come along and not make trouble."

Quincy grinned. "You've got nerve, brother. What crime am I supposed to have committed?"

"Warrant says attempted murder on the person of one Joe Bledsoe."

"Who made the charge?"

"Matt Ames. He brought Bledsoe in last night with a slug in his arm."

"So that's the way of it! Bledsoe and Ames try to dry-gulch me, then they accuse me of murder when I fight my way clear!"

"I ain't the court," the messenger said with a shrug. "You can talk about it at the trial."

"There won't be any trial," Quincy told him. "Not while

a drunk and a crook run Machete law. Take back the warrant and tell Naylor to put it where he'll always have it with him."

The deputy didn't seem flustered. "They're offering a reward for you, Quincy—dead or alive. I'm giving you the chance to make it the easy way."

"Who's offering the reward?"

"I didn't hear."

"No matter. Maybe you tried to do me a favor but the answer's the same. I'll stand trial for the shooting of Bledsoe at the same time that I lodge a charge of attempted murder against him and Ames. That will be when somebody else runs Machete's law. Not before."

"There's a lot of men willing to try for that reward."

"I suppose so. Probably some of them armed by the sheriff—like Bledsoe was—with guns supposedly impounded as evidence. Well, tell them that we'll shoot any man who tries to come around Rock Corner. That's all!"

The deputy didn't argue further. He took his flag back around the outcrop, no one speaking until he had disappeared. Then Quincy turned to face his backers. "Looks like they've put the outlaw stamp on me. That means the rest of you get it if you stay with me. I'll not ask any man to take that risk. You can pass the word to the others. Now's the time to pull out if they want to go."

"I'm real scared," Applegate drawled. "Havin' spent four years bein' a Rebel I reckon it won't hurt me none to put in some time bein' an outlaw."

That drew a laugh and Quincy felt better. At least he was going to be sided by men who didn't scare easily.

They waited for perhaps twenty minutes without seeing anything more of the enemy. Then a head appeared, followed by two others, the men creeping into view when nothing happened. Quincy watched until he saw that the advancing men were calling back over their shoulders to others who were still out of sight. At that point he said calmly, "Knock some splinters of rock down on them, boys. Let them know we're here but don't draw blood."

Applegate's rifle banged with the last word. The other two fired a split-second later, all three stopping to laugh at the hustle displayed by the retreating deputies.

"Looks like they got the point real sudden," Morgan chuckled. "Maybe they'll listen to good advice next time."

The afternoon was waning fast, and as they watched the rock Quincy tried to guess what would be the next move. Obviously it was likely to be a desperate one. The mere business of offering a dead-or-alive reward for a man who had not been proven guilty of anything was a blatant declaration on the part of Pacific that they were willing to buy the murder of the man who was blocking their plans. It was just as obvious that they thought they could get away with such an outrage because they had already bought the local law. Having declared themselves to such a degree it was not reasonable to expect that they would have any scruples in the future.

"Morgan had better stay here with Applegate," he said at last. "We've got enough track in to make good our claim, even though the show has turned into something a lot different from the legal battle it shaped up to be in the first place. As of now we forget legal claims and prepare to defend ourselves and what we now hold. Miranda, you come along back with me and pick up a load of grub. A couple of you can move camp right down here in Fort Applegate. Jase will take command and set up the watches. I'm going up to the rim."

They grinned broadly at his name for the little pile of boulders and he started back up the gorge with Miranda beside him. They talked it over as they walked, and once more Quincy had the feeling that Jules Miranda was a man of some depth. He already had learned that the dark-faced fellow had served for some time with the Louisiana Tigers during the war, but he had a suspicion that he had not been just another soldier. Like many another man on the frontier Miranda evidently preferred to avoid discussing his own background and Quincy was willing. It was enough to know that he had on his side a person of some intelligence.

It was decided that Snedaker should go up with Quincy to the rim, thus putting four men on guard for the night up there. The rim camp was more open to attack than was the gorge, so the extra man could be used there. Fritz would have to remain on duty at the block and tackle, ready for any quick moves which might be necessary.

Snedaker and Fritz agreed to the plan without argument and within five minutes Quincy was on his way to the summit, Snedaker following him as soon as he had cleared the first set of riggings.

There were four men instead of two on the rim when Quincy arrived there, the newcomers being a brawny pair of young fellows who looked enough alike to be brothers. Both were big, blond and ruddy, neither of them over twenty-five. Muldoon introduced them as Ned Harkrider and Sandy Barbour, explaining that they had been doing odd jobs for various homesteaders but were anxious to earn the better pay Midland was offering.

"You'd better hear what I've got to say," Quincy told them. "Maybe you won't want to take the risks that go with that kind of money."

Harkrider exchanged a knowing glance with his companion. "We ain't much scared," he stated. "There's plenty other ways of gettin' hurt around this neck of the woods. Long as we can fight back we're satisfied."

"You're hired then," Quincy agreed. "If Muldoon says you're all right that's good enough for me. So far he hasn't picked a wrong one."

The night passed without incident. Having five men in addition to Quincy in the camp made it easy enough to keep an alert guard on duty, and at dawn pickets went out into the timber, scouting with particular care along the lower rim. There was no sign of any move on the part of the enemy.

After a quick breakfast Quincy issued orders, first following out the suggestion Applegate had made. The mules and the wagons were moved a good half-mile upstream to a point where the slope hinted an end to the main barrier of the ridge. There was a chance that the Pacific forces might try a flanking movement, but if they did it would be aimed at the rim camp and would probably not cause them to stumble on the picketed animals. Nor was that part too important. Quincy wasn't intending to go anywhere.

All supplies had been unloaded before the wagons were moved, of course, and they spent a good portion of the morning moving food and ammunition to the canyon floor. Everyone understood that they were digging in for a real siege but no one seemed to worry about it. The game now was to fight for time, hoping that the Midland lawyers would get something accomplished in the state courts.

The day passed as peacefully as had the night. Applegate sent up word that Pacific was moving in on Rock Corner with their construction work. He had scouted cautiously and believed that they were preparing to blast the big rock. That would pose a new problem, Quincy realized. With the rock gone the defense of the gorge would be a lot tougher for a small defense force.

He tried to guess how long that defense might have to hold. Back in New York they had estimated that the lease matter might drag out for another month or six weeks. Ten days of that time had already passed when he arrived in Machete. That had been the twenty-second of April and today was May fifth. Almost another two weeks gone. A decision might come any day—or it might drag along for another fortnight. He didn't dare let himself think what it would mean if the decision should go against Midland.

Figuring it out that way made him realize how desperate Pacific would be getting. Unless they had the state courts as completely under control as they did the Elk County machinery they must know that their lease would not last much longer. They had to break through into Devil's Canyon before the order came. Otherwise they were losing everything.

Quincy ordered all men into guard positions. Another hundred feet of track had been wedged into the rocks at the base of the south wall, but that was as far as he intended to go. It was enough to hold the gorge. From now on the important matter was to keep control of that one little stretch of wood and iron, whether any more was built or not.

That evening they discovered that the enemy had not completely forgotten them. Just at dusk a rumble and clatter filled the canyon, the men at the bridge dashing for cover on the north side of the river as boulders began to tumble down the abrupt south cliff, Quincy was in the rim camp when it started and he sent his men to the edge in an effort to locate the party that was rolling the rocks. In the gloom they could see no one, and in a few minutes the rock slide subsided.

At dawn on the following morning the enemy resumed the attack. This time Quincy kept two men out on patrol while he and Morgan sniped at the fringe of trees where the rocks seemed to be starting. This sort of thing might be merely a diversion to hide an attack on the rim camp and he didn't want to be caught napping.

Again the onslaught was of short duration and when it

was over Quincy went down on the ropes to see what it had meant.

"No damage," Snedaker told him with a tight-lipped grin. "Most o' the dornicks jumped clean over the ledge into the crick. One big one smashed a pile o' ties but we needed some more firewood anyhow."

"Nothing hit the bridge or the track?"

"Nary a one. Seems like a man can't aim a rock real good from that high up. They take some real funny bounces."

Quincy didn't comment for several minutes. He was squinting down the river at Rock Corner. Finally he said, "Seems to me like it's time we gave those polecats a real dose of their own medicine. Have we got a good supply of dynamite in camp?"

"We got most everything," Snedaker laughed. "That O'Hara sure sold us a big bill of goods."

"Lucky us," Quincy murmured. "Take a look at the upper cliff just above Rock Corner. Do you think the right kind of charge might knock off that lip so that it would fall into the gorge?"

Snedaker's grin spread as he studied the ledge of rock which projected above the big outcrop. "Seems like," he agreed. "Is it square above the big hunk?"

"I'll go see. Who's a good dynamite man around here?"

The New Englander frowned. "I thought you knew. Miranda."

"Yes? I hadn't heard that about him."

"Rebel explosives expert. Mined Vicksburg and such places."

"Fair enough. Maybe he'll be just the man we need. Otherwise I'll do the job myself."

He headed downstream without another word, studying the rock formation as he walked. The idea was simple enough. The canyon defense would be more difficult when and if Pacific should blast Rock Corner out of the way. The obvious way to replace that valuable barrier was to drop another one in its place. While Pacific prepared to blast the big rock at the bottom of the cliff Midland would get ready to blast an even bigger one at the top.

He found Miranda and Applegate playing Casino behind the rock fort, neither of them paying particular attention to the distant clank of metal on stone. They left their game as

Quincy came into view but their interest was on the recent rock rollings rather than on the affairs at Rock Corner.

"It's just another of the attacks we've got to expect," Quincy reminded them. "Attacks which might come at this point as well as from above."

Applegate grimaced. "We ain't as careless as we're act-in'," he said. "No more'n an hour ago I snuck around the corner to have me a look-see. Them fellers is drillin' holes all around that big rock. Long as they're figuring to do a big blast job it sure wouldn't make sense for them to try no other kind of attack till the blast goes off. So we save our strength and eyesight."

Quincy laughed. "Sounds like smart reasoning. Now tell me what happens after the blast goes off."

"Then we got some hot stuff to handle. They'll move on us in force."

"We'll need more men then," Miranda added quietly.

Quincy shook his head. "At that point we withdraw from this fort. I think there is another way without exposing our men to either the blast or the attack." He explained his plan and it met with instant enthusiasm. Miranda hesitated only momentarily before asking, "You want me to do it?"

"I understand that you know how."

"I have done such things."

"Then this one is yours. Head on back to the tackle and get your stuff hauled up to the rim. I'll send somebody else here to be Applegate's army. Anybody you want in particular, Jase?"

The lanky man scratched his chin thoughtfully. "You might send young Eddie Morgan. I always could beat the daylights out of him playin' Casino. Now that he's makin' good money it seems like I ought to cash in."

"Morgan it is. Don't take him for too much."

"I'm a real soft-hearted critter."

"I imagine. How far do you think Pacific's blasting operation has got to go?"

"Hard to tell. Jules took a look and said they wouldn't be bustin' anything up for two-three days yet. Awful lot of rock to blow out of there."

"Let me leave a warning with you. I know this man Kell and if he's up to his old habits he'll use twice as much dyna-mite as he really needs. Try to keep a watch on matters around the bend. When they get ready to make the blast you get far back up the canyon. Otherwise you might get caught in one of his pet earthquakes." Then he added, "If our part of the plan works out you'll have to leave anyway. We'll work that out later."

He followed the hurrying Miranda back toward the rock chute, keeping a good hundred yards behind. He wanted an opportunity to consider the war-like preparations he was now ordering. It was a real reversal of his earlier plans, but there didn't seem to be anything else to do. He had been under direct personal attack and his camp was getting the same treatment. If the enemy wanted to make a war of it they ought to get as good as they could send.

Midland's position was pretty good, Quincy decided. They were subject to attack from the rim or from beyond Rock Corner; otherwise the position was a snug one. Since the rim was the more vulnerable point it would require more men for defense. In order to spare men for the rim they had to make the job easy for Applegate in the canyon. It was as logical as that.

They held a brief conference at the foot of the chute and within the hour the Midland forces had been re-deployed. Morgan and Applegate were the only guards left in the gorge except for Dutch Fritz, whose duties as middle man at the rock chute removed him from the list of fighting men.

The afternoon was pretty well gone when Quincy assembled his little army in the rim camp and explained what was to be done. The camp itself was placed in a more defensible condition, the natural rockiness of the ground being utilized to build suitable cover spots for individual riflemen. Then they began the chore of hacking away the timber that surrounded the spot. In the event of a mass attack there was no point in encouraging an enemy by providing cover for the assault. It was not a particularly cheerful thought, but none of the men seemed to worry about it as they plunged into the work.

Chapter 16

At dusk there was another rock-rolling attack from across the gorge, Midland riflemen breaking it up with rifle fire. At dawn there was a repetition with the same result. Evidently the enemy wanted to knock out that bridge.

"We'll not worry about the bridge," Quincy told the men. "That piece of track is our claim to the canyon. Be ready to do a bit of sniping if you see anybody skulking around over on the other rim but don't let them distract you too much; it's not that important."

Along with Miranda and Snedaker he left the rim camp as soon as the men had breakfasted. Muldoon was to take charge of the regular defenses, paying particular attention to the business of clearing away the brush from in front of the camp. Miranda had made an early-morning scout along the rim downstream, reporting that there was still no sign of enemy activity in that area.

"Seems like they might be planning to concentrate everything on rushing our position in the gorge after they blast Rock Corner out," Quincy said thoughtfully. "We'll figure it's going to be that way. Have to gamble one way or another and this seems like the best bet."

The three of them moved southward beyond the chute with considerable care, skirting the edge where they dared to approach it and keeping an eye open for enemy scouts. In many places it was not possible to see down into the canyon itself but after about a half-mile they found an overhang where they could work out to the very edge and look down.

"About two-thirds of the way," Quincy commented. "If we can find a spot like this just above Rock Corner we'll be lucky."

They were lucky. When they found another spot where they could see the river they seemed to be directly above the bend. The ledge on which they were kneeling ought to

be the overhang they had spotted from below. It was really
a long slab of solid rock extending out beyond the ragged
rim, a few straggling piñons having found precarious root-
holds in its crevices. Fifty feet back from the edge there
was a deep break which seemed to extend all along the rim,
although that part could not be checked because of the
way the crack had been covered with accumulated soil and
humus.

"Think you could knock off the whole mass by putting
your dynamite down into this crack?" Quincy asked
Miranda.

The dark-faced man nodded. "Good chance. Let me
take a closer look."

They spent a good half-hour in working out the details,
but when Quincy left them he felt sure that the job could
be done. Erosion and ice action had cracked the rock
pretty badly at that part of the rim, and it seemed likely
that the big slab was none too securely anchored among
less stable bits of stone. It would take a lot of dynamite to
move it, but the job ought to be effective.

Back at the rim camp Quincy reduced the guard and
timber details long enough to draft the two newcomers into
the job of hauling dynamite. The three of them proceeded
gingerly through the pines to the spot where Snedaker and
Miranda had been digging out the crevice.

At dusk the job was done, everything connected with it
being well hidden from the view of any scout who might
come up on the rim. Quincy felt pretty good about it when
Applegate sent up word that Pacific's blasting crew had
been drilling hard during the day, obviously forcing the
pace as they prepared to open the way for an attack on
Midland's outpost.

There were no more rock-rolling attacks, either at dusk
or dawn, and it seemed likely that Pacific was getting ready
for a big push in the gorge. That suited Quincy well enough.
The rim camp was not as easy to defend as was the canyon, so he much preferred to have the enemy strength
concentrated below.

At dawn he sent Harkrider down into the gorge with a
careful set of instructions for Applegate. The other men
on the rim fanned out as scouts. Quincy took up his position on the first rock overhang they had noticed on the
earlier exploration. From it he could even see part of the ac-

tivity in the Pacific camp. It seemed certain that Applegate's report had not been exaggerated. Pacific was getting ready to blow Rock Corner out of the way.

Then something seemed to go wrong down there. At the distance Quincy could not tell what it was, but there was a definite show of disorder. At one stage the blasters seemed to be on the point of taking over, the drill crews moving back. Then the change took place and the drill men went back to work. Probably Kell having a hard time making up his mind, Quincy thought. In spite of his haste Kell would want to make the blast big enough. Here was one spot where he could really let himself go.

The rest of the day began to build up tension. Midland wanted delay, but every hour of delay on this particular stage of the show merely added to the risk. Midland was ready; Quincy wanted Pacific to force the issue before any Pacific scout could stumble upon the defense preparations.

Another peaceful night passed but no one slept very much. There was too much tense anticipation in the camp, men sharing Quincy's anxiety to get this plan worked out before an accident could expose it.

They went back to their chores at daybreak, Quincy watching the enemy camp from his rock ledge. There was a bustle of activity down there, at least a hundred and fifty men involved in the complex preparations. The sight made him realize how much his own crew needed the rock barrier in front of them.

A little after ten o'clock he saw the drillers pull back. Tiny figures still hurried along on the ledge east of the big rock and he could guess that they were laying the fuse. It seemed to be a long job, and he understood why. Jeff Kell was going to slice off a big chunk of rock with this blast. It had to be a big one.

When he was sure that the time was approaching for the shot, Quincy shouted a warning to Miranda and began to push small rocks over the edge of the chasm. Up here on the rim timing would be important so he wanted Miranda and Snedaker ready. Down below the key word was Safety; the falling rocks would be the signal for Applegate and Morgan to pull back up the gorge.

He listened for several minutes to the dwindling clatter of the falling stones and presently he caught the faint crack of a gunshot. There was no sign that anyone in the Pacific camp had paid any attention to the sound, so Quincy was satisfied. That was Applegate's acknowledgement of the rock signal.

The area below Rock Corner was being cleared of men now. "Get ready!" Quincy shouted to Miranda. At the same time he raised his hand above his head, looking up to make sure that Miranda could see him.

He watched narrowly, holding his hand high until his arm began to ache. Then he saw a Pacific man light the fuse and duck for cover. Quincy's estimate was going to have to be pure guesswork. He waited a few seconds and then signaled Miranda. The minutes then ticked slowly by and Quincy held his breath.

Luck was with them. It was impossible to distinguish between the two explosions in terms of sound or rumble, but from his vantage point Quincy could see both. Far down along the edge of the river a piece of the solid cliff seemed to deflate slowly and collapse in a cloud of dust and splinters. At the same time a huge piece of rock separated itself from the upper wall and began to plunge down the steep incline, turning slowly as it fell. The odd part of the whole picture was the amazing slowness with which it all seemed to happen.

Snedaker and Miranda ran across toward him. Quincy grinned a reply to their unspoken questions. "There she goes! From below they'll never even suspect that their own blast didn't loosen it."

By the time the big rock reached the lower level it was part of a tremendous rock slide and the observers on the rim could not tell very much about the real results. The canyon was full of rock dust and they could only guess that their blast had sent its debris down into the right part of the gorge. At least the rock slide and the lower dust cloud had merged, so perhaps the job had been accomplished.

"We'd better get away from here," Quincy said after studying the dust for a few minutes. "I don't suppose it makes too much difference if they find out we've outguessed them, but I'd still rather have them think that they played in bad luck. No use attracting too much attention to this rim. Bring in your equipment. Don't leave any odds and ends around for their scouts to find."

It was just past noon when he arrived on the floor of

Devil's Canyon. Fritz reported that Applegate and Morgan had gone back down the gorge to rebuild their shattered fortifications. The blast had been terrific in the lower canyon, starting a dozen small slides. There had been no impression of a second blast on the rim; it had all seemed like one huge explosion.

Quincy could see the success of his ruse long before he reached the spot where Applegate and Morgan were rebuilding their rock redoubt. Rock Corner was no longer a solid barrier but it was still Rock Corner, a sloping pile of granite slabs and chunks extending out into the stream until the Boulder was beginning to rise a little above the narrow funnel that had been formed. Pacific could put their crews to work on this mess and would be kept busy for some time. Eventually they would be able to clear the way for an advance, Quincy knew, but the blast had bought valuable time for the defenders, maybe as much as three or four days.

He said as much to Applegate and the lanky man nodded agreement. "How much more time have we got to win?" he asked. "Seems like even a Yankee court hadn't ought to take all year on a little thing like a busted lease."

Quincy shrugged. "They told me it would be a month or six weeks. Not more than that. I think it was the eleventh or twelfth of April when I got that estimate."

"What's today? May seventh or eighth, ain't it?"

"May ninth. Three or four days could do it—but we can't figure that way."

"Then we'll figure more," Applegate chuckled. "We-all ain't goin' nowhere nohow."

Fortunately the other men agreed with him. Pacific spent a full week in clearing the largest boulders of the barricade, leaving only the upstream rocks that served to protect their working parties from any possible Midland sniping. Applegate's little guard party made no effort to interfere. They just sat back and watched, waiting for the moment when enough of the rock would be hauled away so that Pacific could move forward with armed men.

There was nothing to indicate that peace could not be expected indefinitely. Pacific evidently did not suspect that the huge rock slide was anything but pure mischance and they did not make any investigation of the rim. For that matter they even stopped sending snipers to the south rim. During the week in which Pacific cleared boulders out of the gorge there was no hostile demonstration of any sort.

The Midland men combined business with pleasure. Scouts on the upper rim managed to do a bit of hunting while they scoured the woodland, and the men in the gorge had fair success at fishing. Quincy encouraged both operations. They could use the extra food and it might keep the men from getting bored with their situation.

On the sixteenth of May he went forward to the spot where Applegate was holding the rebuilt fort alone. From the rim he had seen how thin the barrier had become. "They're hauling the stuff away pretty fast," he told the lanky man, but they're fixing it so they don't move anything that shows on this side. My guess is that they want to break through suddenly and in a big way when they make the break."

"Stands to reason they would," Applegate replied. "I was just thinking that if I was boss-man over there I'd make the last move durin' the night. Likely they could be thinkin' the same way."

"Could be tonight," Quincy said. "They're cleaned up pretty good on the other side."

At daybreak next morning there were four Midland men in the stone fort, all of them uneasily aware of the opening which now appeared in the rock barrier. Pacific had done a lot of work during the night, operating quietly enough so that the roar of the river concealed the sounds of their work.

"Mighty near cleaned out," Applegate said after studying the bend for several minutes in the gathering light. "But I still ain't seen hide nor hair of nobody."

"Getting organized, I suppose," Quincy growled.

Applegate vaulted over the rock wall and headed down the gulch. "Then I want to see what's what," he called back. "It makes a difference whether I'm stayin' here to face a rifle attack or some more of that dynamiting."

He didn't get very far with his intention. When he was only about fifty feet from the stone fort there was the crack of a rifle from the bend. It was followed almost instantly by two other shots, and Applegate turned to beat a hasty retreat. In the stone fort Quincy picked up one of the spare rifles to draw a bead on what he took to be a head well up toward the top of the remaining pile of loose rocks. Pacific had planted snipers in several hiding-places among the boulders.

"You hit?" he asked Applegate as he jacked another shell into the chamber.

"Nope. Heard some nasty whistlin' though. Got them polecats spotted?"

The lanky man was back behind the wall now, peering out through a crevice. "One up high near the place where the cliff begins," Quincy said. "I took a shot but I don't imagine I got very close."

"Another one to the left of the big spiked hunk of the openin'," Morgan stated. "I made him duck in a hurry."

"Looks like the battle is joined," Quincy said grimly. "From now on we fire at anything that moves. Don't let them do any work there if you can help it."

He stayed with the outpost all day, taking part in the sporadic firing which was the pattern of the fight. At dusk he knew that they had gained another twelve hours at the expense of some fifty cartridges expended. So far as he could tell there had been no injury to either side. That part suited him well enough. The big difficulty was that there was no good way to keep up such a stalemate during the night.

Another dawn told him how the enemy plans were going. During the night Pacific had done two things; they had widened the opening through the rock pile and they had pushed forward with a stone rampart that now faced the Midland fortification at a distance of less than fifty yards.

Again the day was spent in sniping, Midland riflemen dividing their time between the men at the Pacific barricade and the occasional workmen who showed themselves at the bend. Pacific's advance base was obviously intended to take the pressure off for the workmen, but Midland's snipers didn't play it that way; they ignored Pacific fire to put a halt to Pacific construction.

Once more the shooting was harmless. At least such was the case on Midland's side and Quincy had no reason to believe that the enemy had taken any harm.

"We've gained a couple of days," he told Applegate and the others at dusk, "but we can't go on again like this. Tonight they'll push their works forward, probably with plenty of men in position at dawn. Then it's a case of a mass assault or a volume of fire that will pin us down completely."

"We can hold them," Applegate said quietly.

"I'm afraid not. The odds are too great and I don't see any point in sacrificing good men in a hopeless cause. I think I've got a better idea."

"We can use one."

"I'll leave as soon as it's full dark. You boys stay here and see if you can't annoy them a bit during the night. At the first sign of light in the sky tomorrow morning pull back at least halfway to the rock chute."

"You mean we're aimin' to let them have it without a fight?"

Quincy shook his head, smiling thinly. "I'm aimin' to send down another hunk of the rim. Maybe we can block 'em off for another week without having to use rifles."

They liked that idea. He let them chuckle over it before he reminded them, "It's got its drawbacks. So far Pacific hasn't paid too much attention to the rim. Once they get the idea that the upper level is the key to the whole situation we may have trouble up there. That's why I held off as long as I could. Now we've got to take the risk of having them transfer their main forces upstairs."

He left them as they argued the point. "Remember now. Get out as soon as you see the first fading of night in the sky. Daylight won't show too early down here so we'll wait for real dawn before we dump the stuff down into the canyon. That will give you time to put up some sign of fight until the last minute. You see, I want Pacific to be back there a piece when it happens. No point in burying men who just picked the wrong party for their employer."

The rim camp had no rest that night. Miranda and Quincy set the new charge of dynamite by guess in the darkness while the other men patrolled the rim as scouts. It was ticklish work out there on the rim, trying to get close enough so that the blast would actually dump a load of rock into the canyon and at the same time not risk falling in ahead of time. Once Quincy felt himself slipping down over what he suspected was a shoulder of the rim but he pulled himself back by grasping a piñon and never knew whether he had been at the edge or just on the side of a smaller hole.

A half-hour past daybreak they set off the blast but were

unable to judge the results since no one could see down into the gorge at that point. In the middle of the morning Applegate sent up a report. The blast had been a complete success. The gorge was once more sealed off, this time at a spot directly across the old line of Midland defense. Applegate's rock fort was completely buried by debris.

Late that forenoon the peaceful period on the rim ended. A Pacific patrol exchanged shots with Midland sentries, and a little after noon there was a sharp skirmish in which the only Midland casualty was a scratch sustained by Eli Snedaker. That was enough to start Quincy off on a new line of concern. He wondered what he would do if he were to be faced with a real problem of caring for wounded men. With the fight shaping up into its present stern form that was something which might have to be considered.

He checked the supplies and discovered that this was one department where the O'Hara and Muldoon foresight had slipped. There were no medicines of any kind in camp. Nor were there any bandages. Snedaker's flesh wound could be taken care of with strips torn from a shirt, the wound itself cauterized with whiskey, but in case of other injuries the situation might become rather grim.

"I'll go to Machete for medical supplies," Quincy told them when they gathered for the evening meal. "Keep an alert guard tonight and watch for me when I come back. Being as there's a reward on my head I might be in a bit of a hurry."

Chapter 17

THEY TRIED to talk him out of it but he wouldn't listen. If he expected men to risk their lives in his employ he had to prepare for emergencies. And he needed to do a bit of scouting.

He made good time down into Machete, meeting no one even after he was slipping along through the alley which led to O'Hara's stable. Within a few minutes he had tied his horse at the corral and was approaching the back door of the house, his only mishap being to catch a clothesline across his neck in the darkness.

A cautious knock brought Margaret O'Hara and for a moment he could only sputter, his vocal cords still paralyzed from the clothesline. The girl didn't ask questions; she simply pulled him into the kitchen, closing the door hurriedly.

"What's wrong?" she demanded when they were inside.

He managed to explain his errand as well as his temporary speech trouble. "It's dangerous for you to have me around, so rustle up some surgical supplies and I'll get away in a hurry."

"You should have sent someone else. Haven't you heard about that reward they're offering? Dead or alive?"

"I heard. How are people taking the idea of their law officer trying to buy the death of an unconvicted man?"

"There's talk. I don't know whether it will amount to anything."

"Any idea what Pacific plans to do about our blockade?"

"That's no secret. They'll bull their way through. I hear that a bad blast stopped them for a while, but they'll go on when the rubble is cleared."

Quincy chuckled. "Maybe we can make 'em more rubble. Any chance of hiring more men?"

"I've already hired the only ones I had in prospect. At the moment they're also on the Pacific payroll, assigned to keep in touch with enemy plans."

Quincy smiled. "You're always one step ahead. Keep them where they are but warn them to lay low if they get into a skirmish. Our boys are shooting to kill from this point on."

"Doesn't sound like the same man," she murmured as though talking to herself. "A few days ago this game had to be played peacefully and on the right side of the law. Now . . ."

"No peaceful way of fighting bullets," he retorted. "I played their legal game and—with your help—beat them at it. They switched games, so I had to do the same thing."

"I understand. I was just trying to be funny. By the way, you might like to know that Mrs. Kell seems to have stuck to the line she indicated that day when she came to you in the store. She seems quite bitter against her husband and the other Pacific men. Maybe she might help you."

She was looking in another direction as she spoke, her manner suggesting that she was somewhat uneasy about her own ideas. Quincy shok his head as he made his reply entirely serious. "Elinor's a smart woman. She may object to Jeff's methods but his success will still be her success . . . and she's still married to him. Don't bank on help from her."

"You think her self-interest will be stronger than her . . . emotions?"

"I imagine so. Brainy women are inclined to be that way. Maybe I'm prejudiced but efficiency like Elinor's has always rubbed me the wrong way. When I saw how Pacific's job was being operated that day up canyon I was almost sympathetic to Jeff."

"You mean you think a woman is not supposed to have any brains?"

His rugged features broke out into a grin. "I'm just pointing out that this was another item where I've had to change my mind. Sometimes it's real handy to have a smart female around. If she's a strawberry blonde it's extra nice. Want to go fetch those bandages now before I talk too much?"

For a moment or two he was afraid she was going to call his bluff—and he wasn't yet ready to have it called. Suddenly, however, she turned away, disappearing into the store and remaining there for perhaps five minutes. When she returned she handed him a couple of snugly wrapped bundles and said quickly. "This ought to take care of you. And I forgot to mention that my father is now at a meeting with Pettigrew and Eadie, the hotel man. I think they're trying to stir up some opposition against Naylor. You'd better get back to your camp before anything starts happening here."

He grinned at the blush that went with the words. "Coward," he said softly. Then he took the bundles and went out, well satisfied with his trip to Machete.

The light-heartedness remained with him on an uneventful trip back to the rim camp, but a dawn attack made him turn his mind to less pleasant thoughts. Heavy rifle fire from the rim south of the camp quickly drove in the Midland pickets and for most of the morning a snipers' battle raged. It was long-range shooting but it kept the Midland men pinned down while the substantial Pacific force dug in. At first Quincy thought they were laying regular siege to his camp but by noon he realized that the enemy was entirely on the downstream flank. They had seized and were fortifying the area where Miranda had set off the blasts.

"To be expected," he told Muldoon. "When we dumped that second load of rock on them they knew what they had to do, and they've got men enough to do it. Now they keep us penned up here and at the same time protect their operations in the gorge. Now we've got to find some other way of buying time."

"How much more will we be havin' to buy?" the Irishman asked.

"I wish I knew. Back East they told me it would be six weeks until the leased track would be returned to our outfit. That time's about up, but I haven't heard anything cheerful on the subject. All we can do is hold on and wait."

They waited, digging in for a night attack which never came. At dawn, however, the new Pacific strategy became apparent when a dynamite blast shook the mountains. The enemy had knocked off a piece of the rim just as Quincy's men had done.

Applegate came up through the chute a half-hour later, relieving Quincy's concern about his safety. "Plenty of time to git out from under," the lanky man drawled. "Takes rock quite a spell to tumble all that distance. But we ain't going to hold that canyon like we been doin'. They got themselves a new shield to work behind—and when they bust through again they'll be right on top of us."

"How much elbow room do you have down there?" Quincy asked.

"Couple hundred yards. No more."

"Hold it as long as you can. We'll do the same up here. At this point we don't have much choice."

"All right if I put a man on the other side to do some snipin'?"

"You're boss down there. Hold any way you can, but don't risk the lives of yourself or your men if it gets hopeless. That's my only order."

The next three days were a continuing nightmare. Reports from the gorge indicated that Pacific was building rail right up to the new rock slide, at the same time preparing to break through that new barrier. The strategy had permitted them to seize almost all of the canyon below the Keyhole and it was obvious that they were preparing a big-assault on the Midland position around the bridge. But Quincy could do nothing about it. He had to stay with the outnumbered defenders on the rim, trusting to Applegate's little crew to delay matters on the lower level.

The third day was the worst, partly because everyone was feeling the strain of the seige and partly because Pacific's fire was heavier than ever. Either they were preparing a full-scale assault on the rim camp or they were trying to cover some other movement. At dusk the battle raged vigorously, although still at long range. It was noisier than it was dangerous, Quincy realized, the only wounds being minor scratches where bullets sent flying rock chips into the faces of the entrenched defenders, but the threat of something more ominous was all too clear. At any hour the enemy might decide to put on the big push.

Suddenly the firing broke off, the silence even more nervewracking than the constant rattle of gunfire. The defenders were getting a respite, but everyone knew that the interval might be only a prelude to something more desperate.

Because he was restless and worried Quincy did not try to sleep but took over the early guard details from two other men, letting the others get badly needed rest. The night was quiet and he ranged far out from the camp in a scouting expedition which proved to be surprisingly useful. It took a long time because he had to use every bit of stealth at his command, but eventually he knew that the enemy had withdrawn his pickets. The rim camp was no longer surrounded. Now he knew that something was due to happen.

What actually did happen was something he had not expected at all. He was working his way back to the rim when he heard a movement behind him. A horse's hoof clanked on a rocky patch. Then other hoofbeats sounded and he could catch a whisper of sound as someone tried to soothe the animal. Quincy waited in silence, knowing that the sound was coming closer. If this was the new move he proposed to sound the alarm before an enemy could get close to the rim camp.

Then he realized that there was the sound of only one horse approaching. Nowhere else in the timber could be heard the noise of other animals or men coming on. It didn't make sense.

He held his position, gun ready, but suddenly he caught an odd note in the whispered orders of the approaching rider. For a moment or two he could not believe his ears but then he called out cautiously, "Is that you, Miss O'Hara?"

The redhead's exclamation was stifled in its first gasp. Her whispered reply was only a little louder than the tone she had used to the horse. "Thank goodness I didn't strike the wrong part of the ridge. Where . . . ?"

"Keep coming. I'll follow you into camp. We're in dangerous territory here."

As she passed him he saw that she was leading her pony, trying to move as soundlessly as possible. "Straight on," he murmured. "I'll cover."

They made camp without incident, awakening only one man. It was Muldoon who roused, his voice half-angry as he realized who was there. Margaret shook off his complaint quickly. "I didn't come because I thought it would be any fun," she said sharply. "There's trouble in Machete."

"What kind of trouble?" The question was practically a chorus between Quincy and Muldoon.

"Naylor's gang must have learned that opposition has been developing. Tonight they arrested the two men who have been leading that opposition—my father and Mr. Pettigrew."

"Arrested?" Quincy echoed. "On what charge?"

"I don't know exactly. Something about conspiracy to overthrow legal authority. The charge won't matter; it's brazen outlawry any way you take it."

"Where are the prisoners?"

"In jail. I think Naylor and Judge Potter tried to make it sound legal. They arrested both of them and held a quick hearing, with no witnesses except the ones Naylor brought in. All I know is that both are in jail with a thousand dollars bail on each.

"And nobody will offer the bail?"

"Of course not. Everyone knows that an offer of bail would only result in another arrest. I think the main idea is to try to smoke out the other people who are sympathetic to our side. Anyway, there's no one in Machete except my father and Pettigrew who could dig up that much money on short notice."

"I've got it," Quincy said shortly. "What else is happening in town?"

She seemed confused by his change of topic. "What do you mean?"

"I mean that we might put one over on them if I went in with bail. I'll have to make the move in some manner that will catch them off guard or they'd simply add me to the bag. Perhaps it could be done if most of Naylor's outfit was busy somewhere else. I've been suspecting that they're up to some new move and it's possible that their move may be the diversion we need."

"There were a lot of them in town tonight. More than usual. You wouldn't have a chance."

"I don't know about that. Can you get me into town without discovery?"

"I think so."

"Then let's go. Muldoon, you take general charge here and keep the guards on the alert all the time. I don't think the enemy is in force on the ridge tonight but they're undoubtedly up to some new move. Be ready for it. I'll try to get back before they start the next show but if I don't make it remember the orders. Resist while there's a chance to hold them. If it looks hopeless don't let the men do anything foolish."

They talked matters over in a little more detail while he was saddling the one pony which had been kept at the rim camp. There wasn't much to say and within a very few minutes Quincy was leading the way back over the trail Margaret had used in approaching the rim. They were unchallenged as they made a cautious trip through the timber, riding at a good rate of speed only when they found the old wagon trail. By that time Quincy knew that they had an excellent chance of reaching Machete unobserved. Naylor had thrown a picket line around the town but in that line were two men trusted by Gavin O'Hara. With such a line on duty it was not likely that other patrols would be out.

Neither of them wasted time on protests after Margaret's first warning that the case seemed hopeless. Quincy simply told her that he intended to do what he could and she accepted the decision without apparent emotion, concentrating on giving him all the information possible. After that they rode in almost complete silence, the girl taking the lead and angling around to the east so as to approach Machete from that direction. She seemed to know what she was doing and Quincy did not argue. He didn't even stop to think that it was rather odd for him to be placing so much confidence in a girl he scarcely knew. In the past she had shown herself to be efficient; that was enough for now.

It still lacked three hours to dawn when they were challenged by a dark blur which they knew was a man on horseback. Margaret answered softly. "That you, Martine?"

"Right, ma'am. Come along." He pulled aside as they approached, his voice dropping a tone or two as he said, "Watch your step at the edge of town. Word's out that Kell's handlin' a new move. Goin' out right after breakfast."

"What kind of move?" Quincy asked. He liked the idea of having the gang out of town for the coming day but he didn't like to think of being away from Devil's Canyon if an attack was brewing.

"Don't know what it shapes up to be," the picket said. "Us fellers on this picket line don't get called out for no other duty."

"Then you haven't heard any guesses?"

"Nope. I ain't talked to nobody since Miss O'Hara rode out."

They went on after a couple of other questions which brought no information. The town was dark and they met no one, going directly to the O'Hara home. Mrs. O'Hara was asleep on a settee, evidently having worried herself into exhaustion without being willing to go to bed. They left her lamp burning, but Quincy went on into an inner room to keep out of sight. Margaret remained with her mother, ready to carry on the role of worried daughter in the event that someone should come.

Nothing occurred to warrant Quincy's attention until just before dawn. Then he heard a cautious knock at the door and a man came in, whispering loudly enough so that he could overhear. The information being passed along was to the effect that all Pacific men had been ordered out. At dawn they were to launch two campaigns simultaneously, one against the rim camp and the other through the gorge itself.

Quincy assumed that the messenger was one of the men trusted by O'Hara so he showed himself to ask questions. The man knew no more than he had already told but he had an impression that this time the attacks were to be pressed hard. Something had stirred up the Naylor-Kell combination and the orders indicated an urgency that was almost desperation.

"Any talk of a report from the East?" Quincy asked, wondering if perhaps the court decision had been rendered and the enemy was trying to win through before it could become general knowledge.

"Didn't hear anything like that," the man said. "Want me to snoop a bit more?"

"Don't do anything that will bring you under suspicion. Go along with your orders and use your own judgment. What has happened in court won't make any difference to what I'm planning to do next."

Chapter 18

MRS. O'HARA awakened just as the man went out, firing a series of questions at Margaret in rapid German. The girl replied in the same tongue, somewhat to Quincy's amazement. It had not occurred to him that she would speak the language but now he realized that it was the most natural thing in the world. German was almost her real language; her excellent English something she had acquired after the German and the rich Irish brogue she sometimes assumed. She was quite an astonishing person in many ways.

His thoughts were interrupted as she turned to translate the substance of the conversation. "My mother and I are going out into the town," she announced firmly. "It's only natural that we should be prompt about trying to do something for my father and it will give us a chance to pick up some information."

Quincy started to protest against the move as dangerous but did not even finish the sentence. It was obviously the reasonable thing to do, the only way to get the information that was needed. With the two women together they would be reasonably safe, even with an armed mob gathering. Margaret smiled quietly as though reading his thoughts and he met the smile with a broad grin. "Go ahead and say it," he chuckled. "Smart women do come in handy sometimes."

She made a mocking little bow. "Thank you, sir. I'm most gratified."

"And I'm duly abashed. I hope it makes you very happy."

"We'll talk about that later. Just now I've got other things on my mind."

The two women went out without further talk and Quincy was left to sweat it out alone. He could hear a lot of movement in the street but he did not risk going to a window. Not only his own safety but the safety of the O'Haras was now at stake. For the moment Margaret had to be his eyes.

Margaret and her mother returned in a little less than an hour with a rather complete report. Sheriff Naylor and Jeff Kell had led two separate parties of armed men out of town a few minutes earlier, every man in each group having been sworn in by Naylor as a deputy sheriff. Naylor's force was understood to be heading for the canyon, while Kell's smaller group was on its way up the mountain. The rest of the town was quiet, most people keeping out of sight.

"What about your father?" Quincy asked.

"He's still in jail along with Mr. Pettigrew and Dan Eadie from the hotel. They must have picked him up during the night after I left town."

"How many men at the jail?"

"Only the ones who were on duty as guards around the

town during the night. They sleep in the back of the jail building during the day. Ten of them, I believe."

"Nobody on duty there?"

"One man. Old Barkis. He's court clerk and general handyman for Naylor and his crowd."

"Fair enough. I want exactly twenty minutes from the time I leave here. At the end of that period you arrive in front of the jail with four horses saddled and ready to go. Understand?"

"How are you planning to do it?"

"I'm not sure. I'll try to make it legal if I can, offering bail. If this Barkis person tries to pull any tricks I'll do something else—but I'll have them on the street in twenty minutes or we'll all be in there together."

"Do you think it's necessary? If the other crowd is showing so much pressure it may mean that they know they're losing. Perhaps we could wait for whatever change is coming."

"That doesn't sound like you. Midland's purposes may be served by waiting, but at this point I'm not much interested in my duty to Midland. I'm much more concerned about the safety of a number of men who have gotten themselves into danger trying to help me. Three of them are here in the jail and the others are out along the canyon. I've got to move fast if I'm to do anything for both groups. Will you be along in twenty minutes?"

"I'll be there. You want guns?"

"For everybody. And now you sound like Peggy O'Hara again, thinking of the details I missed. I'm walking to the jail. Less conspicuous that way."

He went out without another word, moving along down the street at a leisurely pace with his hat pulled well down over his eyes. There were few people on the streets and no one seemed to pay any attention to him. That was one point in his favor. So many strangers had been in town lately that he was being accepted as just another Naylor hired gun.

The sheriff's office was closed up tight, so Quincy turned in at the courthouse, finding the place deserted except for a little bald man whose pink sleeve-garters gave him a rakish appearance that was notably at odds with his otherwise mousy personality.

The little man looked up without apparent recognition of the visitor, but his eyes widened as Quincy slapped a stack of bank notes on the counter which ran across the front of the office. "Here's bail money for O'Hara, Pettigrew and Eadie. I want them out without any delay, and I also want a receipt for this money. When the Governor sends in state officers to take over this rat's nest I want to know what happened to the cash; there's not going to be any more fancy tricks by that thieving sheriff!"

He hadn't intended to say all of that but the startled expression on the clerk's face suggested that he might be ripe for a good strong bluff.

"The . . . the state's takin' over?" Barkis gasped after finding a bit of trouble in getting the words out.

"Of course. You didn't think a thief and a drunk could run things forever, did you? If you're smart you'll save as much of your skin as you can."

The little man surrendered abjectly. "Put away the money. I ain't signin' nothin' that'll hook me up with this mess. Go ahead and take the prisoners."

"With you, my friend. You don't look dangerous but I'm taking no chances. Get your keys and lead on. I'll be right behind you—ready to get tough."

It was ridiculously easy after that, the bald man even cautioning Quincy against a noise which might awaken the men who slept in a wing of the courthouse. Within five minutes the three prisoners were back in the clerk's office with Quincy, helping themselves to weapons from a closet pointed out by the very much cowed Barkis.

"What now?" O'Hara asked when the first details were attended to.

"You tell me," Quincy retorted. "We'll have horses for all of you in a few minutes. I'm on my way out to give the men at the gorge a hand. You know the local situation better than I do, so you make your own choice."

He went on to fill in what he knew of the situation, getting an unexpected assist from the bald man.

"Kell's planning to blast your men off the rim while Naylor wipes out the others," he stated bluntly. "They know they got to get rid of every man who could give evidence. Then they can claim everything as Pacific's."

"You mean they plan to kill every Midland man?"

"Sure. That message told 'em enough to make them desperate. If'n they don't wipe your crowd out today they'll never get another chance. The state boys ought to be showin' up by tomorrow anyway."

Quincy tried not to show his astonishment. No wonder his bluff had been so effective. He had called the turn exactly. He merely nodded toward O'Hara and the others. "You see what I've got to do. If Pacific knows that I'm not in the trap they'll realize that there's no point in trying to wipe out the others. If I can let them know in time I may be able to save bloodshed."

"I'm goin' with you," O'Hara stated. "These fellers can take care of the town. Eadie, ye know what's what. Get a gun and go back to the bunkhouse. Git your men awake without rousing the others if you can make it. Then you can lock up the one what might stir up a ruckus. I'm leaving it up to yourself how to handle it."

Quincy grinned at the tone of command. Sergeant O'Hara was taking over his squad.

Pettigrew spoke sharply. "Hold it a moment. There's somebody coming up the street."

"Likely Margaret O'Hara. She's due here with the horses in a minute."

"Coming the other way. Three men and a woman."

Quincy pushed forward and saw Elinor Kell galloping toward the jail on a big black horse, followed closely by three strangers. He motioned for the others to remain quiet, watching until the quartet halted in front of the courthouse. Then he stepped out into the open, his hand on his gun.

"Come on in," he invited dryly. "You can tell us what the present excitement is about."

No one seemed to note the veiled threat in his words or manner. Elinor Kell fairly tumbled from her saddle, her expression a little hard to read as she exclaimed, "I'm glad you're here, Jack. I've just learned some terrible news. Jeff must be stark, raving mad to be doing such a thing."

It took some little time to untangle all of the facts but eventually the various bits of news sorted themselves out into a decent pattern. The three men with Elinor had just arrived in town on a special train. They had authority to take full charge of local government in Machete and had already moved into action to the extent of seizing the telegraph line and putting armed guards on the railroad property. For the moment their half-dozen deputies could control the town, but they had wired for militia to take care of a possible brush with Naylor's gunmen. The legal battle was over and Pacific had been counted out. That information had come over the wire on the previous evening, but Kell and Naylor had suppressed it in order to make a final desperate bid for victory.

"Just what is Jeff trying?" Quincy asked the distracted woman.

"I don't know. I understood that he was simply pushing construction work. It wasn't until the telegraph operator talked to these men that I even suspected him of the things he evidently has been doing. He's mad, I tell you!"

"We'd better hear this from the beginning," one of the state men cut in. He had already showed Quincy his credentials as a member of the Governor's military staff. "We knew we were coming into a dirty mess, but it begins to sound like attempted mass murder."

"You picked the right name," Quincy told him shortly.

"What can we do?"

Quincy outlined the situation as he now understood it. "You men can get down into the gulch and stop the gang there. Let them know their cause is hopeless, and you ought to get a quick surrender. Most of them are hired guns and they won't risk their necks any more than they need to. I'll undertake to stop the operations on the summit."

"How many men do you want?"

"I'll go alone. You can't afford to weaken your hold on the town. Keep matters under control here. Send only a messenger up the canyon. That way we don't risk a fight that might mean danger to a lot of innocent people here in town. The important thing is to let the Pacific gang know they're already licked. They won't put up a fight if they know it's all over."

He left the group as Margaret O'Hara rode up with the horses, ignoring their final shouts and answering the girl's question only with a suggestion that she talk to the others. Then he was riding hard out of town. With everything in such a terrific mess it might be a long time before organized action could develop. With the situation what it was in the Elks he could not afford to use that time.

He kept his bronc at a steady run even after taking the upgrade. It was a killing pace for the horse, but Quincy didn't hesitate to force the pace. Human lives were hanging in the balance and if necessary the horse would have to be sacrificed. He followed the trail part of the way to the summit, cutting across then to save a little time and distance. It was hard going but it might save a few minutes and at the same time permit him to move in on what ought to be the rear of Kell's line. Twice as he approached the rim he heard sharp exchanges of gunfire and the sound was reassuring. Muldoon and the others were holding out.

He was still some little distance from the skirmish when he broke out into an open patch just as three riders appeared out of the timber on the opposite side. There was an instant for him to recognize Ames, Winters and a third man he recalled seeing in the canyon. Then he was pulling his tired horse into a sideways lunge as the trio opened fire.

The horse skidded, then stumbled, and Quincy realized that one of the first enemy shots had found its mark. He kicked loose from the stirrups just in the nick of time to roll clear as the horse went down. For a moment or two he had all he could do to avoid the threshing hoofs of the wounded pony, but then he had his gun out and was fighting back. The three men had come straight at him, apparently scenting an easy kill, and their move gave him a decent target.

It was no time to remember his intention of avoiding bloodshed. He had to kill or be killed. A slug tore at the crown of his hat but he held steady to knock the unidentified man cleanly from the saddle. A second shot turned the others but he didn't think he had scored a hit.

He held his fire as they swung away but almost immediately realized his mistake. They were not retreating, merely pulling away to reload. It gave him a similar opportunity but he sacrificed it for an improved position, scrambling across to shelter himself behind the body of the now motionless horse. By that time they were coming on again, both of them low along their horses' necks.

He ignored the whine of a pair of slugs, drawing fine on the vicious hatchet features of Jerry Winters. He squeezed the trigger and the face disappeared. Two horses thundered past and almost over him, one riderless but with the other man pumping lead down at him as he went by. Quincy ignored the thrust of pain in his leg just as he had forced himself to pay no attention to the ugly sound of bullets smashing into the body of the horse. It wasn't a matter of being brave; it was simple desperation. He couldn't let himself do anything else.

He twisted around to throw a shot at the retreating Ames. It was too low, he knew as soon as he fired it, but the gunman's horse stumbled and threw his rider headlong. Ames landed in a rolling fall, scrambling to his feet and diving into the cover of some piñons.

The respite permitted Quincy to reload and to examine the wound that was turning his trouser leg into a bloody mess. He could move the leg so he decided that nothing was broken. Then another slug whined past his ear and he rolled back to his belly behind the dead horse.

"Stop it, Ames!" he yelled. "I came up here to tell you that it's no use. The state has taken over. You can't gain anything by any more shooting."

The reply was another bullet, this one so close that he believed that he could feel the wind of it. A little patch of smoke showed among the trees so he banged an answering shot. If Ames wouldn't listen to reason he would have to dispose of Ames. Otherwise he would not get to the scene of the main action in time to stop it.

They exchanged another pair of shots and this time Quincy's effort brought a howl of pain from the enemy. "Lay off!" Ames shouted. "I give up."

Quincy was not taking chances. "Then come out with your hands up."

Somewhat to his surprise the burly man obeyed. He was holding his left hand high but the right hung limp at his side. Quincy still didn't move. "Get that other hand up!" he ordered, squinting along the barrel of the Colt.

"Don't be a damn fool!" Ames yelled. "Your stinkin' luck-shot paralyzed it. Shot the gun right out of me hand."

"Fine," Quincy told him. "Just keep right on coming. Now! Stop and turn around."

Again Ames obeyed and Quincy pulled himself erect, gritting his teeth against the pain in his leg. He closed in cautiously, aware that Ames was beginning to wiggle the fingers of the right hand. "Stupid luck-shot!" the man was grumbling. "Didn't bust nothin' though."

"You're luckier than the other two. Move along there and we'll see if anything can be done for them."

It was something of a relief to Quincy when he found both men quite dead. He knew that he was being callous about it but neither of their lives counted for much, only representing further delay when precious minutes had already been lost. "Take me to Kell," he ordered his prisoner. "If you're smart you'll do what you can to help me. The jig's up for your gang and there's no point in letting anybody else get killed."

Ames went along silently, still wriggling the fingers of the partly paralyzed hand. Quincy gritted his teeth against the pain that was now shooting through his leg, refusing to look down at the wound because he was afraid of what he might find. There just wasn't time for bandaging, even if he had dared to take his eyes from his prisoner.

Once the burly man looked back, grinning at the sight. "Stopped one, did you?" he grated. "I hope it was me that got you."

"Keep moving and don't . . ."

He broke off as his good ankle turned over on a loose stone. The injured leg refused to take his weight and he went down in a heap. He was off balance for only a couple of seconds but it was enough for Ames. The stocky man whirled instantly and kicked, sending Quincy's gun spinning into the timber. The kick did its work but it also gave Quincy a chance to get his good leg under him, ready to meet the next attack as Ames bored in, the clenched right fist indicating that the man had quite recovered from his disability.

Chapter 19

QUINCY'S CHIEF emotion was anger rather than fear. He knew that he was in no physical condition to do battle with a brute of a man like Matt Ames, but personal risk was not the big thing now. This was just a delay, perhaps a permanent one, which would prevent him from reaching Kell in time.

He dodged sideways as Ames bored in, avoiding a roundhouse right and countering with a solid smash to the belly. The blow brought a grunt and a curse but didn't even slow the big man's attack. Ames simply came in again, showering his lamed opponent with heavy punches that broke through Quincy's best defense. Both men were landing damaging blows, but it was Quincy who had to back up, trying to clear his head a little.

Ames tried to follow up his advantage but this time he only feinted with a big fist, kicking instead. Quincy saw the heavy brogan coming up in an arc and managed to twist just enough so that he caught it on the hip instead of in the groin. Even then the shock of it almost knocked him down and once more Ames bulled in.

Quincy got his good leg under him for the instant that permitted him to send a solid smash to the mouth and this time Ames went back. Quincy hopped in pursuit, hammering with both fists in a desperation assault. He did plenty of damage while Ames was off balance, but then the stocky man closed in a clinch that was like a bear hug. They swayed madly for a moment or two, Quincy still pumping short but powerful blows to the bewhiskered face of his enemy. Then they went down with a crash, Quincy on the bottom.

The fall knocked most of the remaining wind out of him but he still contrived to avoid the knee Ames was trying to use. The pressure on his ribs was agonizing as the burly man clamped on the hold, so Quincy stopped hammering and reached for a choke grip. Both men were fighting silently all the way, Ames trying to break the taller man's back while Quincy kept his stranglehold with his left hand and hammered at Ames's face with his right. The only sound was the thud of the blows and the gasping of lungs being assailed doubly by alkali dust and enemy effort.

Quincy never quite knew when the pressure on his chest began to relax but after what seemed like an eternity of pain he realized that Ames was weakening. He hammered all the harder, still keeping his choke-hold. Suddenly Ames shifted his hands, trying to rip Quincy's fingers from his throat. At that same instant Quincy got the leverage he wanted and drove home a real punch to the enemy's chin. Ames grunted just once and rolled over.

It required a good two minutes for Quincy to get to his feet. Then he used another valuable bit of time in getting his unconscious enemy tied up. The firing ahead had dwindled down to little more than sniping fire and the sound of it told Quincy that somehow the situation had changed. He guessed that his own men were now pinned down hard, kept there by those occasional enemy shots. He didn't like to think what it really meant.

He didn't take time to look for any of the fallen weapons but plunged straight into the timber, dragging the wounded leg behind him. It took a good five minutes for him to make a painful hundred yards but then he saw men in front of him. At that moment a bullet clipped the piñon just beside him so he went down in a hurry, shouting, "Send Kell out here. This is Quincy. I want to talk to him."

He could sense the hesitation in the enemy lines. There was no firing for quite a while and he yelled his message again. "Send Kell. Stop the fighting. It's all over. The Governor has sent state men to take charge."

Again there was a delay, but presently Jeff Kell's voice rang loudly. "I'm coming, Quincy . . . and I'm coming armed!"

Quincy didn't reply. Even talk was now getting to be an effort. He rested for a moment and then used his neckerchief to bind the bloody trouser leg hard against the wound. For the moment it ought to help stop the flow of blood.

By that time Jeff Kell was coming through the piñons, a fierce excitement showing in his eyes. Elinor had been right, Quincy thought; the man was insane.

"Who's with you?" Kell demanded.

"I'm alone. Jeff, you've got to call off this crazy attack. The state troops will be here pretty quick. Don't make things worse for yourself."

Kell's sneer faded into a frown that seemed almost sincere. "You're hurt, Jack. Bad?"

"Not too bad. Don't worry about it. Just get your men back and stop that shooting. You can't save anything now but lives."

"No rush, Jack," Kell said, his voice oddly smug. "Let's see about that wound. You're losing a lot of blood."

"Forget the blood. Order your men out."

Kell didn't even reply. He pushed Quincy down and went about the business of dressing the wound, which proved to be a clean gash across the fleshy part of the leg. Twice Quincy tried to argue with him but Kell paid no attention. The firing had ceased completely so Quincy let well enough alone, nausea over the handling of the wound making him too weak to protest anyway.

Finally it was completed and Kell stood up, smirking again. "Honors of war—and all that sort of rot," he sneered. "Just like they do it in the heavy romances—only this time I fooled you. This was the delay I needed."

Quincy couldn't even phrase his question but Kell explained without waiting. "I sent word to your men that you had ordered a truce. That's why the shooting stopped. Meanwhile my boys have been finishing up the blasting preparations. In another minute or two it'll all be over. Your stupid louts will never know what hit them. Nobody will be left to talk but our side, and we'll swear the blast was your work. Naturally I'll have to kill you too. Neat, eh?"

Realization of what Kell's show of kindliness had meant brought Quincy to a sitting position. "You're a fool, Jeff! My men and I aren't the only ones who know the truth. Everyone in Machete knows. The state has taken over! Don't you understand that?"

The sound of hoofbeats broke in on Kell's reply and he swung to aim his gun in the direction of the sound. To Quincy's amazement it was Margaret O'Hara who drove an exhausted horse into the clearing, almost trampling him before she could pull the staggering animal aside.

"You were in time!" she exclaimed, ignoring Kell's gun. "I was afraid——"

Quincy interrupted. "He won't believe me. He's all set to blast the upper rimrock down into the gorge!"

Her eyes went wide with horror. "Your wife, Mr. Kell!" she gasped. "Your wife is down there. You mustn't let it happen!"

He was staring numbly at her, his gun hanging limp in his fingers. She seemed to realize that something was wrong with him for she snapped her words sharply at him. "The state went to arrest your men. Mrs. Kell was afraid there would be useless fighting. She thought she could get them to surrender. When she rode up the gorge she said that she would bring out both lots of men even if she had to ride all the way into the Midland defenses—something nobody else would be able to do. She must be down there right this minute."

Shocked realization replaced the mad cunning in Kell's eyes. He faltered for just an instant but then turned and ran, shouting orders at the top of his voice. A single voice shouted distantly from somewhere back the rim but they could not hear anything from any of the men who had been in the lines surrounding the Midland defenses.

"Can he stop them?" Margaret asked, her voice a husky whisper.

Quincy shook his head. "Maybe there's a chance—thanks to you."

Kell was out of sight now but they could hear him yelling his warning, still with no apparent replies. A couple of gunshots banged from the region of the Midland defenses and then the earth bucked under the force of a tremendous explosion.

"Too late," Quincy yelled above the roar of the blast. "Take cover."

He crawled into the partial shelter of the fair-sized pine, pulling the girl down with him. They held the position until the rain of shattered rock ceased, neither of them taking any injury. Then Quincy got his good leg under him. "Let's see how bad it is," he said shortly.

Margaret ran toward her exhausted horse, the animal having been too used up to run when the blast occurred. She brought it back without a word, helping Quincy into the saddle. Then they started through the broken trees, both of them still a little numb from the concussion.

Almost immediately they could see the effects of the blast, the piñons shattered and broken as though by artillery fire. Margaret led the fagged horse around the worst of the debris and presently they could see ahead of them the area of major damage. Everywhere the trees had been flattened as before a giant scythe and in the center of the destruction a huge crater gaped bare and forlorn. Quincy stared in amazement, words failing him for a few moments. Then he gasped, "The rim! It didn't go down!"

Suddenly he realized that men were moving toward him, their leader a gaunt fellow who waved the others out into a skirmish line. "Applegate!" he exclaimed. "Kell didn't get either the camp or the rim with his dynamite!"

He could see his men moving out into the timber with

rifles held at the ready but there was no sign or sound of firing. Then Applegate was grinning up at him, gaunt features dirty and blood-smeared.

"Looks like they skedaddled," the Arkansan commented dryly. "All but maybe three-four, that is."

"Any of our boys hurt?" Quincy asked.

"Two. Neither of 'em bad. Mostly we kept our heads down and let 'em waste ammunition. I kinda had a idea that was what they wanted, just keepin' us down while they set up their blast."

"I suppose it was. Why are you grinning about it?"

Applegate spat carefully, shooting an apologetic look at Miss O'Hara as he did so. "We let 'em have their way;" he said, "only we kinda steered 'em a mite, sorta encouragin' them to put their charge a respectable piece away from our lines and the rim. After they lost a couple of men they seemed right willin' to take the hint. I reckon yore friend Kell seen the mistake when it was too late. He come bustin' out of the woods just as she went off ker-bamm!"

Quincy didn't bother to explain Kell's real reason for making his belated effort to stop the blast. It was enough to know that another Kell dynamiting job had been a failure. The rim camp had not been wiped out and the rim itself had not been knocked into the canyon.

"What happened to Kell?"

"Blast got him. I don't reckon we'll even find no pieces."

"Maybe it's just as well. State authorities are taking over in Machete. Thanks to you and the other boys—and this young lady—we're over the hump. Devil's Canyon will carry Midland rail."

It was something of an effort to get out the final statement. Both Jase and Peggy came to him swiftly as they saw him begin to totter and he was soon stretched out on the ground, the girl pillowing his head in her lap.

Applegate grinned at the scene but his voice was serious as he asked, "Hadn't I better call in the boys? Them Pacific gunnies must have lit a shuck outa here soon as they set off the blast."

"You issue the orders," Quincy told him with a tired smile. "You're in charge." Then he added with a somewhat wider grin, "You're boss—but I'll lay you odds you start getting orders from a certain meddlesome female. Put up with it if you can; she's smart."

Applegate almost choked on his quid as he stammered, "A feller could git bossed around by a gal like her and not mind a dang bit." His bow toward Miss O'Hara was quite a production.

"Perhaps Mr. Quincy didn't mean me," she told the Arkansan. "Maybe you don't know it but he's quite impressed by the capabilities of another lady."

Jase shook his head. "I know what you mean, ma'am, but I'm figuring it different."

Quincy closed one eye in what he hoped was a sprightly wink. "I'm figurin' it just like you-all, Jase," he drawled.

Then he closed the other eye.

Ballantine brings you the best of the West— And the best western authors